Pied Piper

Keith Stuart

Cover artwork and design by Simon Wadsworth

First published in Great Britain by LMP in 2021
ISBN 978-1-913306-15-1

This is a work of fiction and all the names, characters, events are either fictitious or entirely fictional representations

Acknowledgements

I know the only people who read 'Acknowledgements' are those who hope to get a mention so, for them, I would like to record some thanks. First, my group in The Letchworth Settlement Writing Class: Elizabeth, for her expertise and direction; Paul and Lesley for their critique and constant encouragement; Dave for helping me unlock it when I was stuck, and ALL the others for the inspiration I get from their enthusiasm and fun.

Thanks to my sons: Simon, for designing the cover and Peter, for reading it and saying he loved it. Mostly thanks to my wife, Heather, for her constant love and patience and for listening to many extracts and re-writes on the way.

Thanks to Len Maynard at LMP for taking *Pied Piper* on and reassuring me that the story has some merit – family and friends were bound to say so but he wasn't.

I should dedicate the book to my wife and sons but, if they will forgive me, I'd like to dedicate it to my Mum. I can imagine her with the book open on the arm of her chair as she reads it whilst simultaneously knitting furiously and watching Coronation Street!

Foreword

On September 1 1939 the British Government began *Operation Pied Piper*, a plan to evacuate almost three and half million children from towns and cities feared to be at risk from German bombing raids. Extraordinarily 1.5 million children were moved in just three days, to places thought to be safer. The first bomb did not fall, however, until almost a year later, by which time many children had returned to their homes.

Prologue

Michael sits alone, gazing across the fields that back onto the garden. Joe had placed the bench at the end of the path for him, so he had always been able to negotiate his way to it. First in his rickety wheelchair, then on his wooden arm-pit crutches and through the rest of his life with his walking stick.

Today is no different, though it took the longest time of all to reach the well-worn lattice bench. He walks slowly, stooped, his coat hanging oversized on his frail body. His shock of white hair ripples in the autumn breeze as he lowers himself stiffly onto the bench, wincing as his knees bend reluctantly. He lived with a particular pain in his hip for almost fifty years almost missing the ache when the joint was replaced with a titanium one. It was an ache which reminded him less of hurt and much more of love and care, fond memories of a time in his life which was at odds with the world beyond him.

Now settled on the bench, he sucks in the soft, clean, fresh air. When he closes his eyes, as always, images of his dad came flooding in.

Chapter 1

I greeted Mary as I came in: the children disappeared while I peeled off my sweat-soaked clothes and lowered myself into the tin bath. Mary had placed it away from the stove, as she always did, so that she could continue preparing the tea. The heavy curtains at the windows sealed us in, trapping the steam from the bubbling pots and the smells of roasting meat and boiling vegetables. Between stirrings and tastings, she gathered up my things and dropped them into the basket for washing the next day.

Each evening I watched Mary prepare our meal and afterwards clear the dishes from tea, all washed, dried and back in the cupboards in her neat, organised way. She has always been trim, tidy, pretty, from the day I first dated her and through the weeks we courted. She bloomed while she bore our children, delivering without fuss or complaint, taking to motherhood seemingly with ease.

She kept the home in the same easy way, and it seemed unfair that I could watch her, admire her skill, wonder at her ability to cook the tea, amuse the children, fill my bath all at once, while she never got the chance to see me at my lathe.

I did a good job at turning the metal, each fine thread dropping to the floor and gathering in pools of shiny shards around my steel-capped boots and beneath the machine. The workshop was noisy. It hung heavy with the tang of metal and oil and sweat so, though I wouldn't say as much to anyone, the sweet smell of washing, baking bread and the special one of the children, was a balm no tin bath of hot water could match.

As always, my bath was ready for me as I walked in through the scullery door. My legs ached from standing all day, my shoulders from the hours hunched over the lathe. The hot September day had made the workshop oppressively hot, a heaviness compounded by the talk of events unfolding in France.

Stories from both reliable and dubious sources told of German soldiers sweeping across that country. Word was thousands of women and children fleeing Paris were dropping like flies in the searing summer heat as they headed for safety in the south. There were tales of summary executions for trivial offences and German fighter pilots using lines of refugees as target practice. Only in the safety of our unofficial workshop-men's-club was fear expressed that, after France, we were next.

We knew the talk of our children being evacuated was about to become reality but, whilst we readily expressed our anger with Hitler and the Nazis, we only reluctantly made mention of our children going away, for fear of revealing how we truly felt. Mary and I could not even contemplate being separated from our sweet, precious children as we sat by the radio each evening, listening to the latest news, official statements preparing us for packing our little ones off on their own.

Mary listened intently, a handkerchief dabbing her eyes, only to cry herself to sleep each night since the plan was announced. I listened from behind my newspaper, hiding my moistened eyes and gently bidding her to stop her crying. 'They'll be fine,' I'd say. 'It might never happen,' I'd try to reassure her but my reassurance convinced neither her nor me and all the time I was crying inside. I could almost feel my heart breaking at the very prospect.

Chapter 2

I broke the silence. "Have you told the kids?"

"Not yet. I thought we'd do it together. I think Alice has got some inkling. Things were said when she was out playing. The Robinson kids are saying they aren't going back to school at St Agnus's but some school in the country."

"Will she have said anything to Micky?"

"I don't think so. If she had he'd be all over the place. I think Alice will cope but he will miss you so…."

Mary broke off and busied herself with a pan on the stove. I swallowed to speak but I couldn't, and we fell silent again.

"Daddy, can we come in now?" Alice's voice called from the hallway.

"Leave Daddy for a bit, sweety." Did Mary want time with me alone or did she think the moment needed to pass before they came back in?

"No, in you come," I called and the two of them bundled through the door. Micky came and kissed my cheek and went straight back to the colouring he'd been doing when I got home, singing tunelessly as he scribbled energetically with his crayons. It was a funny ritual the children always observed and never questioned: they left the room while I undressed and turned their backs when I finished, stood and wrapped a towel round myself. But when I sat in the bath, the water was accepted as covering me enough. It was nothing to do with them seeing the scar from the accident at work, simply appropriate modesty.

As she always did, Alice made straight for the bar of yellow soap on the saucer set on the floor beside the bath and she began to rub it on my hair. The feel of her little fingers working up a lather, and her giggles as she made my hair stand up in soapy peaks, just as I had done to her so many times, was almost too much to bear. I wondered when I might feel this again. How long could it be before I would enjoy again this combination of Alice's laughter, Micky's singing and Mary's constant, caring, loving presence.

"Lean forward," Alice instructed so that she could rinse my hair. I so much wanted time to stand still but the bath water was cooling, the tea was bound to be almost ready and I knew I could not defy the inevitable. I leaned forward and put my hands over my face as if to keep my eyes from the soapy water about to cascade from my hair. In fact, it was to hide my weeping which I fought to keep silent.

"There. All done." Do children repeat *everything* you say to them, I wondered. I hoped not. I was always careful not to curse within their earshot, but I did catch Micky practicing "Bugger" under his breath after I had caught my thumb with a hammer one day. It was hard to decide whether to tell him off or chuckle to myself but, eventually, I decided on a compromise. "Secret naughty word, Micky. Not to be repeated," I emphasised by wagging my finger at him. "Certainly not when Mummy or Alice can hear." He had looked at me to check if I was really cross: he knew, and we shared a conspiratorial wink and smirk and he never repeated the word. To my knowledge.

"Daddy. All done!" Alice repeated. "You can take your hands away now." But I couldn't. Not quite yet.

Mary took the towel from the rail hanging by the stove to catch its warmth and, without even checking the children's gaze, I stood, my hands still over my face, and felt the warm, soft towel being wrapped around my waist. I had to take it and tie it, so I managed to wipe my hands down my face as if shaking off the bath water rather than the tears and took the towel. Micky was head down over his drawing and Alice was spreading a cloth on the other end of the table. I stepped out of the bath onto an old, greying towel Mary had placed there. Though the water had cooled the room felt colder and I dried as quickly as I could and dressed in the clothes Mary had laid out on the chair.

I hoped a sense of normality would be restored and I was determined that the next part of our daily ritual of family chatter and laughter round the tea table, would be just that. Normal, safe, comforting. I thanked Alice for washing my hair so well and went over to admire Micky's picture.

I waited for him to look up at me, to hear the approval he knew he would get but wanted, nevertheless. But he continued to scribble. A house, with the two stick grown-ups I had seen in many Micky masterpieces of picnics and playground visits. And the two stick children who also always featured. But unlike in every other picture I had admired with excessive praise, these children were neither holding the grown-ups' hands nor being pushed by them on swings, throwing snowballs at them or sitting with them on a picnic blanket. These two stick children were outside the house, walking down a charcoal black path, gas mask boxes round their necks and cases in their hands.

"Right, Buster, teatime. Clear your things away." He hadn't looked up at me and I hadn't been able bring myself to comment on the picture and, in that split second, he had told me he knew. and I told him I couldn't deal with it. Not aloud. Not just then.

Chapter 3

The next few minutes' thoughts were drowned by the clatter of pots and cutlery and plates but there was an unusual absence of chatter. Alice and Micky always had something to say, correcting and contradicting each other about things they had been doing together and interrupting each other as they shared what they had done alone, each certain the other was being given too much time to tell. But that night they were subdued, quiet.

"Right, you two, hands washed quickly," and I whisked Micky off his feet towards the sink, trying my darnedest to tickle his ribs and illicit a giggle. Instead, he twisted in my arms and threw his arms round my neck, pressing his warm little cheek against mine and whispered in my ear. "I don't want to go, Daddy." I wrapped him in my arms and clasped him so close I wanted him to melt into me so we couldn't be parted.

"I know, Soldier, but it won't be for long and you're a lucky thing getting extra holiday in the country. Wish I was coming." He could never know how much I meant that. "And you have to look after Alice, too, 'cause you know what she's like, she won't want to go either."

Alice could not have heard the exchange, but she sensed the moment and came running from the sink and crashed into my legs, trying her best to join her hands round my waist and bury her face into my belly. I could feel her shoulders heaving with her sobs and, clutching my son in one arm, I reached down and clasped the back of her head and pressed her closer still. Without looking, my eyes were so tightly shut they hurt, I could see in my mind's eye her soft, golden hair, tumbling in bubbling curls half-way down her back.

When I dared open my eyes, I found myself instinctively looking straight into Mary's. She made no sound as tears slid down each side of her face.

"Right, you silly lot. This won't do. We've got tea to eat and lots of getting ready for your adventure. You gotta choose the things you want to take, then everything's got to be packed, Mummy's got labels to write. And I…well I've got things to do, too."

"What have you got to do, Daddy?" It was Alice who managed to join me in breaking the moment.

"Now that's for me to know and you to find out. But you won't be finding out till tomorrow."

"Oh Daddy, that's not fair. That's teasing and you say we shouldn't tease." Micky had eased his cheek from mine and was looking straight at me.

"Yeah, but I'm a grown up and I'm allowed."

As I lowered Micky to the floor again, I kissed the top of Alice's head and inhaled as deeply as I could. I needed to lock in the smell of them both. We took our usual places at the table, Mary nearest the stove to fetch and carry, the children either side and opposite each other, and me at the end opposite Mary. It had never been decided that this is how it would be, it just happened. It was a bit like the colour of eyes, or the size of feet being handed down, inherited. It was just the way we did it and it felt right and comfortable. It was the shape of our perfect little family.

Tea was eaten more quietly than usual: the questions the children must have had I suspect could not be asked. They were too big, too difficult to voice because then they would become real issues instead of potential ones. Neither Mary nor I could guess their thoughts for certain and feared we might sow a seed of fear they might not have had if we were to explore the possibilities with them. So, we sat in a cloud of denial. Not lying to each other by saying but doing so by not.

Micky looked the most lost in his thoughts. It wasn't right that such big things had to be considered by one so small. I daren't even try to put myself in his place, wonder what I would have felt like at six years old, leaving my Mum and Dad to go off to who knew where, to live with who knew who, for who knew how long. One thought poked itself into my head but, as the possibility of never seeing my little ones again flitted across my thoughts, Micky spoke and a shutter seemingly came down and 'what ifs' returned to 'what now?'

"Can I take Bunners?"

In all the magnitude of the situation, in a mountain of potential consequences, Micky's troubled, almost tearful fear that he might be separated from his beloved, stuffed and threadbare rabbit broke the silence at last. And I laughed. It was so absurd, so incongruous and had I not laughed I would most certainly have cried.

My reaction caused the exact opposite of what I would have wished for, however, and Micky dissolved. But he was not sharing the laughter with me: instead he collapsed into silent sobs. His little face broke, his shoulders heaved, and the tears flowed down his reddening cheeks. Alice glared at me, her bottom lip quivering, but she seemed determined not to cry. Mary chose the third option we have when we are at the extremes of emotions. Me laughter, Micky tears, Mary anger.

"Now look what you've done!" she said, staring the length of the table at me. Her words and voice wanted to be angry but her eyes conveyed no such feeling. "Stop it!" she tried and placed her hand to her mouth. But it was no good. Soon she too was giggling. Alice looked from me to her, trying to work out exactly what was happening but the sight of us both giggling in a way she might with her friends if one of them said "bottom" she too caught the infection. She tried to hold her first laugh in but in doing so the force came down her nose instead, bringing with it a bubble of snot.

Mary squealed her mock horror and disgust, throwing her hands in the air. I could only tilt my head back and release the heartiest howl of laughter. The room was filled with a cacophony of Alice's trilling giggle, Mary's babbling laughter and my half-stifled roar. Eventually I lowered my head and wiped the tears from my eyes with the back of my hand. There was a blurry Micky looking from one of us to the other, his mouth agape, clearly certain that the madness of the world had finally reached to the very heart of his family. His sobs had ceased and now he just looked bewildered.

"Micky!" I cried, pointing to his sister. "Look at Alice's snotty nose!" And the dam broke totally. The four of us disintegrated into shaking, rocking, stomach-clutching paroxysms of laughter triggered at the wrong time for the wrong reason about the wrong thing and it was just right.

Chapter 4

Quiet descended after our hysteria and the meal continued more normally. It was as if, at least for a while, we were able to set aside our different fears. We all avoided speaking of what was to happen the next day and, even later, as we stuffed their little cases with as many of their things as we could, we treated it as we imagined preparation for a holiday would be. The children went to bed at their normal time, Micky clutching Bunners under his chin and Alice sucking her thumb. We sat with them longer than we would normally, Mary and I swapping from one bed to the other to share our time with each of them.

"Love you to the moon and back," I assured them both and Micky responded with his, "Twice round the world and back again." I swear I could actually feel a pain in my chest as I sat on the edge of the bed. In my head I still fought between defying the advice and keeping them at home with us and how I would feel if they stayed and something were to happen to them.

Mary and I finally, and only when they had both drifted to sleep, reluctantly crept from the children's room, leaving the door slightly ajar.

In the dull light of the living room we looked again at Leaflet No 3 from the Lord Privy Seal's Office to check that we had done everything correctly. In its efforts to be reassuring it only made us feel more unsure.

"The transport of some 3,000,000 in all is an enormous undertaking. It would not be possible to let all parents know in advance the place to which each child is to be sent but they would be notified as soon as the movement is over."

Not knowing where they were going heightened the worry we already had. We were placing the greatest trust in people we neither knew nor might ever know. The children were going to places away from the cities to where the bombs were unlikely to fall but all they knew was life in the city: playing in the streets, crowded, familiar buildings, the bustle and noise of town life. Neither of them had seen a cow or a sheep for real. Surely, they would feel lost, even *get* lost, in the wide-open fields and woodlands.

Would the people who took them in understand Micky's attachment to Bunners? How would they deal with the occasional wet bed he made: it was not something for punishment with us, just a matter-of-fact thing that we dealt with. Will they laugh or be irritated by Alice's little Miss Busybody stage, her practicing for motherhood and being a perfect housewife? Like her mum.

Still more, will they be together? The thought of them not being so was too awful to contemplate

Chapter 5

As Mary and I lay together that night, just a sheet over us in the sultry September darkness, I feared speaking. If I voiced my thoughts, I knew I would reveal the depth of my sadness and there were already three souls in my life for whom I had responsibility – I could not add my despair to theirs. Mine had to stay trapped inside. But it caused a heavy weight which, at that very moment, felt too great to carry. Mary's arm reached across my chest and pulled me closer to her.

Our lovemaking was always a joyous celebration of our devotion to each other but momentarily I thought it could not be right that night. Yet all emotions are just a whisker apart from each other and we did make love, quietly and gently as we always had to with the children in the next room. Lewd comments had been made at work about enjoying time without the kids, of doing it in every room of the house as often as possible with as much noise as the neighbours would allow.

Most of us joined in the banter which became progressively ruder and explicit but it was sheer bravado, cover for what was really going on inside us. It came to a sudden and embarrassed stop when one of the men declared a particular ambition, something too private to have said even within that brotherly band. He blushed after he'd said it, but he was rescued by the foreman chivvying us back to work. How odd that the emotional tension had so loosened the tongues of friends who wouldn't normally ask advice from each other about treating a boil on the back of your neck, let alone sharing the intimacies of the bedroom.

Mary fell into a restless sleep, but I lay on my back, staring into the darkness. My eyes would not close, sleep refused to come, my mind bouncing all manner of possibilities around my head and all of them featuring my two precious children, lost, sad, anxious, confused and alone.

Eventually I rose from the bed and pulled on my drawers which I had dropped on the floor beside me. I looked in on the children who both still slept soundly, before making my way downstairs to the scullery. I put the kettle on the stove and stood looking through the window onto the street outside and the identical houses opposite. The scene was washed grey by the early dawn and it was still, quiet and confusingly peaceful.

While the kettle boiled, I lifted the latch on the back door and padded barefoot to the privy out in the yard, returning to find Mary, wrapped in a cotton dressing gown, pouring the boiling water into the tea pot.

"I couldn't sleep," I said as I wrapped my arms around her. "I didn't mean to wake you." She turned and smiled but said nothing. She put milk into the cups, with two spoons of sugar added to mine, and poured the tea, leaving the shiny, dark brown tea leaves in the strainer.

I wanted so much to tell her how I was feeling but all she needed to know was that I cared. Nothing more would help either of us. For a mother to be separated from her children was impossible for me to imagine and I could not burden her with my feeling of loss, which could surely not come close to hers.

Mary carried the two cups and placed them on the little table beside the sofa. She checked that her gown was pulled decently round her before she sat and then I settled beside her. Just a few hours before we had been naked and intimate together and yet now we both checked that we were appropriately covered.

"You okay?" I broke the silence.

"I'll miss them so…" Mary's voice broke. "So much."

"I know. Me too. But they'll be fine and the bombs dropping would scare the fu …" I stopped myself: this was not the workshop, no matter how angry I felt. "Scare the hell out of them. They'll be safe and sound. And once we know where they are, we can write to them. You never know, Alice might even be persuaded to write back!"

"I hope they're not cross with Micky when he wets the bed. He does try not to, and you know he's worse when he's worried or if he's not well."

"He'll be fine. He's not the first six-year-old to wet the bed and he won't be the last. I wet the bed in various ways until I married you."

Mary slapped my leg. "Don't be rude."

"Did you write the labels?" I knew Mary would have done this meticulously, but it was a detail which I thought would assure their safe arrival to wherever it was they were going. "Are Miss Morris and Miss Telford going with them?"

"They said some teachers would be travelling with them and helping at the schools where they're staying. That'll be nice for the kids: a familiar face.

We'll see when we get to the station in the morning. Are you coming with us?"

"I can't, Mary, can I? I have to be at work by seven and it says you're not to be at the station before nine."

Truth be known I was glad of this. How in God's name could I wave my children goodbye as they slid away from me, along the platform in billowing clouds of steam. I already had an image in my mind's eye of their tearful faces pressed against the carriage window, the palms of Micky's hands on the glass, either side of his tear-stained face and Alice holding him, comforting him in her too-soon grown-up way. I couldn't bear to see that for real. And I could bear even less the thought of them going off without a care. How selfish was that?

We sipped our tea and Mary rested her head on my naked shoulder, our legs pressed against each other's. We may both have dozed and when I jumped awake, I glanced at the clock on the mantelpiece. It was almost six o'clock. I gently lifted Mary's head from me and whispered, "I'd best get dressed."

"I'll get some breakfast and make your sandwich for work."

I climbed the stairs and looked into the children's room. Still, they slept on, so much more peacefully than their anxious parents. Micky lay on his back, almost starfish, the top sheet pushed off him. His stripy pyjamas were soaked and clung to him and the sheet beneath him was marked with a dark, wet circle. Alice's sheet was also pushed away but she lay on her side, knees drawn almost to her chest, her thumb still comfortingly in her mouth.

I knelt on the floor in the sliver of space between them and put a hand on each of their beds.

"You look after each other, my little sweethearts," I whispered. "You have no idea how much I'm going to miss you every second of every minute of every day you're gone. You make sure you come back to me safe and sound." It never even crossed my mind at that moment that it was they who were leaving us, in a place which was neither safe nor sound. Lost in the sadness of our separation I had not given a thought to what might happen to Mary and me while the children were away, or what they might come back to. All that was in my mind was the disruption to their lives, not what was going to happen to ours.

It said in the Leaflet about the evacuation, *"If we were involved in war, our big cities might be subjected to attacks from the air, at any rate in the early stages and, although our defences are strong and are rapidly growing stronger, some bombers would undoubtedly get through."* How little did we know or understand? Would the munitions we were making at our factory really be a match for Hitler and his marauding army and his reputedly invincible air force?

I hoped so but I feared not.

Once I was dressed and back downstairs Micky was already there, rubbing the sleep from his eyes with one hand and running the other through his hair which stood comically at all angles. Mary had heated some water and was putting some into the tin bath.

"Come on, Soldier, let's get you out of those jim-jams," I said, lifting him to stand in the bath, his feet just covered by the warm water. Mary washed him, gently bridging the gap from fast asleep to wide awake with sweet nothings I couldn't quite hear.

I sat at the table and chewed on a hunk of bread and butter Mary had put on a plate for me, alongside another cup of tea. I glanced again at the clock to see I had only minutes now before there would be a bang on the door and Nobby's voice would be calling for me to "get a move on or we'll be late". I desperately needed time to stop.

Now washed and wrapped in a towel, Mary lifted Micky from the bath and sat him on my lap. "Hello, Soldier," I whispered. "Who's a lucky boy today? Off on your holidays, eh?"

He lifted his head and, with eyes now nearly clear of sleep, he looked at me and smiled.

"I'll go and wake Alice and say goodbye to her," I said almost to myself, lifting Micky from my lap and setting him down onto the chair to wait for his breakfast.

Alice slept on and I used the excuse of not having the heart to wake her to only rest my hand on her silk soft hair and whisper, "I love you, princess," and kiss her cheek.

Chapter 6

Back down the stairs I had to get out of the house: I was sure something was going to burst inside me, and I had to avoid that or at least have it happen somewhere else, somewhere private. It was as though I was holding my breath. Back in the scullery I ruffled Micky's hair as I kissed his cheek, kissed Mary just the same, picked up my flask and greaseproof-wrapped sandwich, strode to the front door and opened it, determined to pre-empt Nobby's banging. Without a backward glance, because I daren't, I said, "Bye, Micky. Be a good boy, won't you?" and stepped outside, gasping for the air.

Nobby and I had known each other since we were infants. We had played and gone to school together, courted in tandem, married within weeks of each other, fathered children at similar times and at similar intervals. Nobby was the first at my side when the lathe broke and fired a piece of shrapnel into my back as I instinctively turned away from it and it was usually me that calmed him when he gasped for breath with his asthma.

We weren't brothers, of course, but in some ways, we were closer than that. We had shared pretty much all that boys and men will share – teasing, jokes, toys, tools, news of successes and failures, events of joy and sadness. Affection was a punch on the arm when we were kids and a firm handshake as men.

But as I closed the door behind me and saw Nobby on the doorstep I could not tell if I needed to throw my arms round him more than he around me. Despite the early morning heat, his cap was perched almost comically on his head, as always. He looked at me with puffy, reddened eyes offering no cheery greeting, no "Morning, Tosser," or some such abusive nickname to disguise his affection. He just looked at me and I at him, and we silently turned to begin the mile-long walk to the factory.

The curtains twitched in the house opposite. Elsie peered out and waved as she always did. I nodded as I always did.

The walk was one we had made together hundreds of times and one we expected to do hundreds of times more. Neither of us was fit for military service – Nobby with his asthma and me with my damaged back from the accident – but the munitions factory was a genuine part of the war effort and we were doing our bit. Yet, for all the frequency we saw each other and walked together to work, day after day, we would talk constantly. We would share things about our children, secretly comparing them to be sure our own were keeping pace or, better still, stealing a march; moan about money, politics, work and, more recently, Hitler.

Wives were mentioned but nothing intimate was ever shared – Mary and Ruth were friends too and who knew what they talked about.

Today we were silent. Not entirely lost in our own thoughts, more sharing them silently with each other because we couldn't say them aloud. Who knows what made us suddenly stop and look at each other? I don't know if I looked at Nobby first or if I became aware of him looking at me, but it seemed to happen in an instant and for no obvious reason. But we stopped. We looked at each other through moistened eyes, smiled an unhappy smile and then walked on, my arm now thrown across my best mate's shoulder.

Chapter 7

"Do we have to have one of these kids, Brenda? I mean it's not like we haven't got our work cut out with the farm and that. And neither of our two are happy about sharing a room, and that's a bloody understatement. Can't we just say we can't have one? It's not like Jerry's started bombing raids yet, anyways."

"Joseph, you know they've said we have to take at least one. We'll just see what we get. If it's a boy, he can share with Bobby and if it's a girl…"

"I know all about that, Bren, but that's not the point. It's another mouth to feed, more washing and ironing for you. They won't know anything about the farm, and I don't have time to spend telling a new kid about all the dos and don'ts. They've talked about rationing food in the new year: do we get more if we have one of these kids? Are they staying that long?"

"Joseph, I know no more than you, do I? Now stop your moaning and let's wait and see. I go down to the Village Hall this afternoon. The train's due about four o'clock and they'll dish the kids out once they arrive. You just imagine what it would be like if it was our two going away."

"Bloody bliss, I'd say. Maybe a swap's possible."

Joseph was already shoving his feet into the boots standing by the back door, then he thrust his cap on his head, his arms into his black tweed jacket and with a "Gonna check the late lambs." He left Brenda pounding the bread dough on the wooden kitchen table, leaving the door open behind him.

"Shut the door, Joe, I don't want a draft." But he was gone, and Brenda moved backwards and kicked the door closed without looking. It was a well-practised action which she used frequently after both her husband and the children. As she attacked the dough, stretching it this way and that, turning, lifting and slapping it back onto the table her mind could wander to all sorts of thoughts in amongst the clouds of flour. Today they were full of the prospect of having another child in the house. Someone else's child. A child they didn't know, from parents they had never met and would probably never meet.

Her own two were not at their easiest now: Beckie was an increasingly awkward thirteen-year-old, straddling uncomfortably the line between being a girl and being a young woman. Joe seemed to find it hard to understand why his little girl had become rather distant from him in recent months and still couldn't understand when Brenda explained that his daughter's monthlies had started, and she was finding it all a bit confusing and embarrassing.

Bobby was a worry to them, and the once little Joseph-duplicate had become a fifteen-year-old rival. His childhood puppy fat had not yet turned to the adult muscle which would make him resemble his father even more and he was still not entirely in control of his rapidly extending limbs. He was randomly morose, childish, loveable, and hard to like.

Father and son locked horns over almost anything and each found it impossible to back down, even when it had dawned on one or the other that he was indisputably in the wrong. Once a willing helper round the farm Bobby had become awkward and argumentative. Just rousing him from his bed in the morning to help with the milking was a battle and, since he'd taken up with the Butlers' girl, getting him home and to bed in the evening was almost as difficult.

It wasn't the best of times to be bringing some city child into the house. It wasn't an unhappy family by any means, rather an ordinary one, in fact, with growing children finding their way. Brenda took the view that, somehow, they could manage one extra for a few weeks, just until the worry about the Germans had passed. But it was hard to know which would be best – Beckie really needed her privacy right now and, though she didn't know quite why, Joseph insisted that Bobby needed his too. It was one of the few times she could remember Joseph standing up for Bobby recently.

At last, the dough was shaped into a smooth shiny ball. Brenda doused the inside of the proving basket with more flour, dropped the solid ball of dough into it, placed a damp tea-towel over it and placed it on the shelf near the range to prove.

She glanced at the clock and reassured herself that her timing was perfect. She had time to rinse her face and hands of the dusting of flour, hang her apron on the hook behind the door, pin her hat to her hair, and head for the village. She needed no coat on this balmy September afternoon, but she took a lavender coloured scarf from the dresser draw in case it cooled before she returned. By the time she got back the bread would have risen, ready to bake and be freshly warm and crusty for tea.

Chapter 8

Brenda couldn't quite take in the scene when she arrived at the Town Hall. There must have been forty or fifty women there, all of whom she recognised and acknowledged with either a nod, a wave or a cheery hello. For the most part it was the sort of gathering she would see several times a year, at the fair, the barn dance, the carol singing, the produce shows. What made this different was the gathering of little boys and girls who stood to one side of the Village Hall door like herded, fearful sheep. She estimated the oldest to be about the age of their Beckie but the youngest looked barely school age. Each had a label round his or her neck and a little box on a strap hanging at their fronts. Some had a small luggage case at their sides, but others clung to them as if they contained something desperately precious and could not be safely set down.

Over the next hour children were allocated to villagers who received them either reluctantly or tolerantly but rarely happily. The accompanying adults were welcomed much more readily by their hosts, but Brenda was glad she didn't get some busybody woman from the city, gate-crashing her kitchen. The gathering dwindled and, in time, just a few children and even fewer villagers remained. Brenda scanned the stragglers and thought that none looked at all suitable for her place – all too young.

Miss Hastings, the village's teacher who had been appointed as the billeting officer and was organising the distribution process, strode towards Brenda, who was now certain she would be thanked for coming and sent away. Joseph would be pleased.

"Brenda, we have a bit of a problem." The woman used the voice of someone needing a stall manned at the fair, a costume made for the nativity play, or some bales of hay donated for the dance and Brenda knew it well. "Agnus isn't well and can't take any of the children and Beryl can only take one. We have a brother and sister and we can't separate them." She pointed to the two children standing hand in hand. "The boy's almost seven and the girl is nine. Do be a dear and take them to your place."

"I can't, Miss Hastings. Both ours will have to share if I do that. It was going to be hard enough to get one of them to. And they're so much younger than ours."

"But you did know that they're likely to be quite young, Brenda."

"Yes, but not two of them. And Joseph won't have it. He's worried about them being on the farm with the machinery and all. And Beckie's being difficult at the moment and you know our Bobby. I can't ask him to share with a six-year-old, can I?"

"We can't send them back though can we, Brenda. I'm sure they'll be as good as gold and, you never know, Bobby might take the little fella under his wing."

Even as the negotiation went on, the brother and sister were being guided by the local constable towards Brenda. The girl looked totally in control, but the little lad looked at Brenda with eyes like an orphaned lamb and, before she could stop herself, she said, "Come on then, you two. You must be starving. Let's get you home and get some tea inside you."

Brenda divided the children and took one in each hand and, without another word, she led them away from the village towards the farm, a mile walk away.

Chapter 9

The day at work had been much as always until the break when the men split, without a word, into two groups: those who'd sent their kids off on the train that day and those who either hadn't got kids or who had defied the advice. I sat with Nobby and we ate our sandwiches and drank from our flasks with hardly a word. As we finished and I screwed the cap back on my Thermos I said, "How's your Julie?"

"She's upset. But I keep telling her not to fuss so. They'll be fine. And we can write to them. And it won't be for long. How about your Mary?"

"Much the same, Nobby."

And that was the sum of it. Even as we walked home, we limited ourselves to comments about news of the Germans in France and little mention of home: we both knew there was going to be a terrible quiet to fill when we got in.

"It's going to be bliss tonight, ain't it. Quiet. Bit of time all to ourselves," Nobby ventured.

"No, it's not, Nobby. It's going to be horrible. See you in the morning."

I sank as low as I could into the tin bath that Mary had filled just a little deeper than usual. It was another warm evening but the difference between the temperature of the hot water and the room meant my protruding knees, chest and shoulders felt chilly. I longed to be able to submerge myself totally and not resurface until Hitler was history.

Mary tried to prepare the tea as if there was someone sick in the house, avoiding the usual clang of pots and pans. But it was the absence of voices that I noticed most. A quiet hung in the room like a heavy blanket sinking lower and lower on top of me. It wasn't the reverent quiet of a church, or the serious hush of a library, but an almost funereal silence. And it was so loud it made my ears ring.

We sat at the table eating without our usual hungry enthusiasm, saying little because there was too much to say. The room was unpleasantly tidy; no crayons, scraps of paper, toys, dolls or clothes. And it was so desperately quiet.

"I suppose they'll be there by now." It was Mary who broke into my thoughts and managed to find exactly where they were. At that very moment I was trying to imagine them somewhere, with someone, unpacking their cases and finding the presents I'd slid down the sides amongst their clothes.

"Probably. But I wish we knew where 'there' was."

Chapter 10

"Brenda, what the bloody hell were you thinking?" Joseph hissed at this wife as they stood by the range, whilst Alice and Micky remained only just inside the backdoor, taking off their coats. "There is no way on earth we can have both of them. You'll have to take the boy back. Or the girl. I don't give a damn which one but one of them has to go back."

"They're not shoes you don't like, Joseph, or broken biscuits. They're a brother and sister, hundreds of miles from home and as likely don't want to be here anymore than you want them. But there was no one else who could take two and you wouldn't want the little mites separated now would you?"

"That's not my problem, Bren. But can you imagine either of our two wanting to share their rooms?"

"No, I can't. I know fine well they won't want to. But they've got no choice in the matter."

"Why?"

"Because on this occasion, I said so."

"Well you can bloody tell 'em, 'cause I'm certainly not."

"I will. Now take the littluns upstairs to unpack while I make some tea and do bread and jam. There's the cot mattress in the loft – that'll be big enough for the little lad. Put that in Bobby's room and the other spare mattress is on the landing already. Put that in Beckie's."

Joseph knew when he was beaten and on matters of the house that was quite usual. With a jerk of his head and a "Come on then", he beckoned the children towards the stairs and led the way.

He directed Alice into Beckie's room. The mattress propped against the wall on the landing was soon flat on the floor of the bedroom and he told the girl to unpack her case and put her things on the bed. He led Micky into another bedroom, and he used his foot to make a path through the clothes scattered on the floor. Brenda had been trying to make a stand with Bobby about at least keeping his room reasonably tidy for her to clean, but he insisted he didn't want her cleaning his room, so it didn't matter if it was untidy. "It will now, Sunshine!" thought Joseph.

Bobby's father risked opening each drawer in the dresser until he found the one least full, scooped the things that were in there out, stuffed them into one of the other drawers and, turning to Micky he said, "There, that's yours. Put your things from your case in there."

At this the boy's eyes filled with tears and his bottom lip quivered.

"Hey, come on, little fella, no tears now. Let's get your case on Bobby's bed and we'll unpack it together, eh?"

He clicked the locks open and lifted the lid. On the top was a well-worn and, therefore obviously much-loved, now thinly stuffed rabbit. Joe handed this to the boy without comment and Micky held it tightly to him while the big man took little piles of clothes out of the case and handed them to the boy, nodding to the drawer. Socks and pants, shorts, shirts and two pullovers. And as he pulled the second pullover out of the case something tumbled from it onto the bed. Joseph picked it up and held it in the palm of his hand. "What's this, then?"

Micky stared, wide-eyed at the wooden car resting in the man's hand. It was perfect: it was carved from wood and smoothed until it shone. The outlines of the doors and windows, lights and bumpers were meticulously etched into the wood. It was as if you could open the doors and climb inside. Each pair of wooden wheels was attached by a metal axle and Joseph showed they went round by moving the toy along his wide, chubby hand. It was simply perfect, and Micky gazed open-eyed and open-mouthed, longing to hold it but fearing it might be taken away.

Joseph smiled and, with the toy resting in his open palm, he held his hand out towards Micky. A barely perceptible nod from the big man gave Micky the confidence to take it in his spare hand and Joseph left the room to give the boy some time alone, to think of home.

When Joseph reached Alice's room, she was also clutching something in her hands.

"Look what Daddy made me," she said as he walked in. She held out the bowl of her hands in which rested the most delicately crafted, tiny little tea set. The two cups, two saucers and two plates, an exquisite tea pot, all, Joseph guessed, from the same piece of wood as Micky's car.

"That's nice, isn't it?" And at that moment Joseph wasn't quite so cross with Brenda for bringing them both back with her.

Chapter 11

The news on the wireless that evening told us nothing new. There was some sort of war going on between our ships and German submarines in the Atlantic; Russia had joined with the Germans in Poland and countries I had hardly even heard of, like Finland and Norway were being invaded and surrendering.

The tone of the news reader was ominous and gloomy. We had already had the war to end all wars and yet here we were, talking of a war affecting the whole world again. A second world war.

But, for all that, nothing was happening where we were. We had sent our children away for fear of bombs raining from the sky and killing us all. And for what? Nothing, that I could see.

It was all a bloody waste of time and the sooner we got the kids back the better. It wasn't right to split families up, send children off on their own to live with people they didn't know. People *we* didn't know. It was mad. Who thought that plan out? They keep telling us it's for the best, that the bombs are coming but what proof have they got for that? None.

Chapter 12

Bobby crashed the back door open and kept it so while he used the boot scraper to get his muddied boots off.

"I wish you'd do that with the door shut, Bob," Brenda said to him, for the umpteenth time but with none of the impatient edge or anger that she would normally. She knew she had to tread carefully in the next few minutes. Bobby was not going to be pleased to find a six-year-old sharing his room, taking up floor space he was accustomed to using as his wardrobe.

"Your bath's ready but I want to tell you something first." Bobby was taking his jacket off and hanging it on the hook behind the door. Here she goes again, he thought. What have I done now? Brenda busied herself peeling potatoes at the sink and launched into her internally rehearsed speech of persuasion.

"You know your dad and I told you we were going to have an evacuee with us? Well, turns out we've got two, see. There's a little girl – she's nine – and there's a little boy, too. He's six, going on seven by all accounts. We had to have the both of them: there was no one else could take 'em. And, well, there's nowhere else he can sleep is there, Bob?" Brenda's peeling became faster, more furious and less precise as she spoke. "Beckie has to share her room with the girl and really there's only your room the little lad can go in. I know it's unfair and you need your own room and all, 'specially your age, and if there was anywhere else... Well there isn't: we can't use the front parlour – there'd be nowhere for you and your dad to have your bath then and it'd be wrong for the boy to sleep in here. It'd be like something out of a Dickens' story, wouldn't it? It won't be for long, Bobby. He seems like a good boy and he'll be asleep before you go up, anyway."

So anxious was Brenda to get all her explaining in without interruption she hadn't noticed Joseph and Micky come in from upstairs. The boy had walked straight to Bobby, who had by then sat himself on a chair at the table to await the end of his mother's tirade, and proudly held out his perfect wooden car. Bobby took it, smiled and mouthed "Wow" whilst his mother continued.

"I don't want you leading off about this, Bob. Your Dad's got enough to worry about without hearing you moaning on."

"Yeah, ok."

"It's not like you don't get time to yourself in the day, while you're working. And you just think how lucky you are."

Bobby had handed the car back to the little boy so that he could have the moving wheels demonstrated to him and pretend to marvel at them. "Yeah, it's fine."

"And you have to be nice to them, Bobby. Just imagine what it would be like..."

"Brenda," Joe interrupted her.

"No, let me finish, Joseph. I'm going to say my piece."

"Brenda!" Joe repeated.

Brenda snapped her gaze from the mutilated potatoes to silence Joseph, only to see her strapping, fast-growing, fifteen-year-old son on his knees on the floor, pushing a wooden car between himself and their new little guest. She looked, open-mouthed, from them to her husband, who merely shrugged his shoulders and said, "Looks like I get the bath first," turned and headed for the privacy of the front parlour.

Chapter 13

Mary seemed at a loose end without the children in the house. There was only us two to feed and only our laundry for her to do. Some of the lads at work dared to admit they were missing their kids whilst one or two maintained their bravado and claimed they'd be surprised if they hadn't added to the brood as a result of the extra time to themselves.

A new routine developed in our lives. The outline shape was the same but the pieces that put it together weren't all there. The mornings were quiet and stressful because they were stress-free. No more chivvying to get up and dressed or queuing for the lav, no more breakfast on the hoof while putting things in front of the kids, and no more circle of goodbyes, ensuring equal shares of affection before leaving, me to work and they to school.

At first the evenings were largely spent in sad silence. The bath routine became merely functional and taken without the tuneless sound coming from the scribbling Micky and the fussing of Alice as she got in Mary's way to help her. I soaped my own hair.

Mary and I would sit in our usual places almost willing the evenings to pass. At a time when we needed each other most, and should have most intimately shared our thoughts, we distanced ourselves from each other. We didn't seize the moment and launch into a second honeymoon and I suspected the other men hadn't either, if truth were known.

At last we learnt where the children were. A letter came to tell us that they were safely in the care of a Mr and Mrs Davies on a farm in Shropshire. Somehow the kaleidoscope of possibilities settled into some sort of picture. That picture in my mind was probably an idealised one of thatched barns, shiny tractors (oh, won't Micky love that), mooing cows and bleached-white sheep but it was a picture which calmed my mind and Mary and I were able to talk more, and share imagines of our children in their new, temporary, home.

I wrote to them:

> Dear Children
>
> Mummy and Daddy hope you are being good for Mr and Mrs Davies. We are sure we do not have to tell you to say your pleases and thank yous. It must be lovely being on a farm and I bet seeing the tractors is good, Micky.
>
> We know you will help in the house if you can Alice.
>
> Having you there is extra work for Mrs Davies. Tell her thank you from us. Be good. See you soon.
>
> Love Mummy and Daddy.

Mary found the time on her hands during the day, time when she would usually have been washing and ironing or cleaning and baking, was making her restless and she suggested that she take some cleaning work. One of her friends had just found she was expecting (turns out one of the lads was true to his word about making the most of the kids being away) but wasn't so good and had been told to stop her cleaning work. Mary offered to take it on. I might not have wanted her to but there was no good reason to say no: the extra money would be nice and, while I was busy enough to take my mind off the worry, it seemed only fair to let Mary do the same.

And so, a new routine developed as the nights began to draw in and we felt the autumn chill. When the November fogs descended to smother the sounds of the city under a thick, choking, smoke-filled blanket, I was glad the children were away breathing clean air.

The work at the munitions factory took on a greater urgency and we were under more pressure to work a bit faster and produce more. The clocking in and out times were watched more closely, and the minutes of our breaks observed with precision. What with the fog, the chill, the work and the absence of the children in the streets, heads remained bowed on the walks to and from work. Nobby and I chatted to each other, but we had fewer notes to compare.

Mary and I, on the other hand, found more to talk about in the evenings. Of course, we were following developments in the war, and the probability of food rationing in the new year was a topic of discussion at work, on the street and at home. But now Mary also had all sorts of tittle-tattle she picked up on her way to and from work and the things she had to tell me about the house where she cleaned made me laugh and feel angry in almost equal measure. How could those with so much complain so easily, and over such trivia, as they seemed to?

Chapter 14

The postman seemed to take some delight in handing the envelope to Brenda having spotted the London post-mark. He hoped it would bring some smiles to some young faces: a few of the village's evacuees had already returned so perhaps the Davies's charges would be going back too.

"Alice! Micky! There's a letter for you," Brenda called up the stairs and they were quickly at the kitchen door. Both children had settled into their new surroundings and whilst Alice was not ungrateful for the welcome they had been afforded and knew she was much luckier than some of the others who arrived at the same time as they, she was envious of those who had gone back home.

Micky was clear in his mind that the ideal solution to it all was for his mum and dad to come and live there: the family restored but in the perfect place.

Alice sat at the table and opened the envelope with a mixture of excitement, anticipation and not a little worry. It hadn't much crossed her mind that anything might happen to her parents back in London because she hadn't allowed such thoughts to lodge there. She knew the bombs hadn't come. But, for all that, she hoped the news was good.

She read the letter aloud for Micky and Brenda to hear and she felt a different mixture of reactions.

At the references to their manners, their helping and the message to Mrs Davies she looked to her and was reassured by her smile and nod. Micky enjoying the farm brought a simple "Yeah!" from him.

When she had finished, she held the letter out to Brenda.

"No, Pet, it's for you two. You keep it. Put it in your drawer."

Still holding it, Alice let the letter rest on the table in front of her and held it a little more tightly, not sure how she felt.

"You can write back later. And you can tell your mum and dad you've both been as good as gold," Brenda added.

Micky scampered off. Alice mulled over that last sentence: "See you soon."

When? she wondered.

Chapter 15

It was strange how those tortuous hours before and after the children left faded in the memory. They say if women remembered the pain of childbirth, they wouldn't do it again and I guess it was something similar. I had paced outside the bedroom door listening to Mary crying out in her confinement and questioned how I could have done this to her. But within weeks there was never a question that she would put herself through it all again. The hurt of the children leaving was huge but, like birth, we knew it was all for something good. The pain ends and you're left with something so very good.

And so, we settled into a different contentment, albeit one which had been inflicted on us. We missed the children no less, but we were able to bear it together. There was nothing more to be said about it and it was a relief that neither was hiding anything from the other; on one hand I no longer battled inside myself about seeming to be uncaring by not showing how I felt and, on the other hand, adding to Mary's grief by doing so.

Nobby and I continued our life-long comradery, but he was suffering from the smog and his asthma was gripping his chest more and more frequently. It distressed me to see him struggling for breath. He had got some sort of contraption supposed to help him get his medicine straight into his lungs, but he refused to take it to work and sometimes I would look across to him in the workshop and see him crouched over, clearly fighting for air.

Mary found solace in being busy and I knew she would be doing her cleaning job with the same meticulous care she took with keeping our house. It would be wrong to say she was happy, but she certainly didn't seem wretched. In the evenings by the fire we would speculate about what sort of day the children might have had on the farm. It was all imaginings because Alice's occasional letters at first said little more than that they were both fine.

Gradually she mentioned how Micky had sat on the tractor, or given milk to one of the calves, how she had made some cakes with Mrs Davies and helped her make the beds. They were both going to the village school for half days, three times a week.

I wanted them to be fine but I'm not sure I wanted them to be happy.

Deep into the autumn, with winter letting us know it was just on the horizon, the smogs became thicker and heavier, the cold and damp more penetrating but there was still no sign of Jerry. There was plenty of preparation going on, though: it felt like someone's justification for sending the children away. Piles of sandbags were distributed along the pavements, the air-raid sirens were tested, blackout curtains were run up on mothers' sewing machines, parcel tape criss-crossed the windowpanes. We were stuck in a frozen state of expectation without really knowing what we were expecting.

Mary got me to go over to Elsie and sort her windows out for her. She'd been on her own since her Bertie died a couple of years ago and she was getting quite frail herself now. I stacked some sandbags on her doorstep, stretched tape across the windows panes and hung some black curtains that Mary had made.

"How are the kids?" she asked when I'd finished.

"Fine. I think."

It was noticeable how few men were around and I wished I had a sandwich board to announce why Nobby and I were still at the factory and not learning how to take apart and reassemble a gun, how to squirm across muddy flats, how to make a bed and get along with others you'd never met or ones you had now met and didn't like.

Women were filling the vacant spaces at the lathes and packing-stands. Nobby and I were convinced at first that this wasn't right and there was no way the women would keep up. But as the days passed, we had to concede that these wives and mothers, expert cooks and housekeepers were well up to this new challenge. The language in the workshop was cleaned up and any occasional slip was instantly followed by an apology and a chorus of a chiding from the men. Truth was some of us had heard the women talking together during the ever-shortening breaks and the topics and language would have made a squaddie blush.

Chapter 16

"Come on, Micky. Get yourself up and dressed. You and me need to get the cows in for milking." Bobby was already sitting on the edge of his bed, mostly dressed and pulling on some thick woollen socks his mother had knitted for him. Bobby had surprised himself as much as his mother and father by how quickly he had become used to sharing his room. He liked the boy's constant wonder at what he took for granted. He secretly enjoyed having someone who clearly liked him and, (dare he think this?), looked up to him; admired him. He genuinely enjoyed the company and coped better than he expected with the forfeit of his privacy: Micky was always in bed and usually asleep by the time he went to his bed, anyway.

Micky's mattress was laid on the floor at the end of Bobby's bed and he was lost, deep down in his blankets, just his hair visible. "Come on, Micky."

"It's too cold."

"Get dressed under the blankets then. Here." Bobby got the pile of clothes Micky had on the previous day and dropped them on top of the sleepy boy. Each piece disappeared under the blankets and in quite short time, after much hidden rolling and tumbling, the boy dared to push back the covers and appear, like a magic trick, dressed and almost ready to go.

It was still dark when the boys had put their boots, jackets and hats on and stepped outside the farmhouse. Joseph was at the kitchen table sipping hot tea and said he would meet them in the dairy as soon as the herd was in.

The co-operative, docile beasts had wandered, as they always did, from their grazing towards the yard gate and the boys had little more to do than open it and let them in. Co-operative and docile as they are, they are also stupid and instead of all walking between the two boys, one or two separated themselves and went to walk outside Micky. Realising their mistake, they corrected their route, but in doing so and moving back towards the main herd, they were going to ignore Micky and squeeze him between themselves and the others.

Bobby saw at the same time both the situation and the worry on Micky's face. "Micky, walk backwards!" he called. The boy was rooted. He knew how to duck a flying football or a cuff round the ear from a street bully, but this was a situation he couldn't work out for himself.

"Walk back towards the gate, Micky."

The errant cows, oblivious to the danger they were creating, moved ever closer to their sisters and Micky was in real danger of being crushed between bovine bellies, or knocked over and trampled on. Bobby daren't cause the animals to panic but he felt sure he had to divert the stragglers again. "Micky, slap that black one's belly. Shout 'shoo'."

This seemed like madness to the boy. Slapping an animal three times his height and saying shoo did not sound like a sensible plan. But if that's what Bobby said then that's what he would do. "Shoo, shoo!" and he patted the flank gradually pushing him into the cow on his other side.

"Harder, Bobby!"

This can't be right, he thought, but now he was becoming genuinely concerned. The space between these huge beasts was diminishing. He smacked the shiny, black belly as hard his hand could manage and the animal almost skipped in surprise, probably at the sound more than the impact, and moved away.

Bobby breathed in for what felt like the first time in minutes. He smiled and quietly clapped his hands at Micky, who looked far less troubled than he should have been.

The cows were now making their way into the dairy and dutifully lining themselves up for the machines where Joseph, who had seen the whole drama unfold, awaited.

When his son came up to him, he put his hand on his shoulder and said, "Well done, Bobby. You sorted that well."

Chapter 17

The bang on the door was early but a little more frantic than usual.

"Just get my jacket, Nobby. Hang on." I waited for the inevitable 'Get a move on,' but it didn't come. Instead another knock. Maybe Nobby was saving his breath. Perhaps it wasn't a good day for him. He knocked again.

"Okay, okay, I'm coming."

With one arm in its sleeve, I used that hand to lift the latch while wrestling to get the other arm into my jacket. The door swung open and I looked up to greet Nobby. But it wasn't him. It was Julie.

"It's Steve," is all she said. Only his mates called him Nobby: to Julie he was always Steve. I knew instantly by the broken look on her face that something was very wrong. I pulled the door to and almost lifted Julie off her feet as I took her round the waist, spinning her and taking the two of us off towards their house, two streets away.

As we walked and jogged, between breaths I asked, "What's he like Julie? Is he bad today?" She would hardly come and get me if he wasn't, but I was hoping that she was over-reacting. Though I knew she wouldn't.

"He was really bad in the night and this morning he just couldn't get any breath at all."

"Has he used his nebuliser thing?"

"Yes. It didn't do anything. He looked so scared."

"He'll be fine, Julie. It's just the cold." My heart was pounding, and I knew from the half walk, half run we were doing that I didn't believe that. I wanted to run ahead but I didn't want to leave Julie.

"What about the kids?" Only after I'd said it did I register what a stupid thing it was to say.

When I reached Nobby's front door, ahead of Julie, there was a moment when I wasn't sure if I should wait for her, call for Nobby to invite me in, rush in and be the first to help or the first to find whatever was to be found. I looked behind me and Julie was waving me to go in: perhaps she was glad I was first.

"Nobby!" I called in as friendly a way I could. There was no reply. I bounded up the stairs two at a time. I knew in this situation it was important to calm my mate down, but I had to do it in an urgent way. Hiding my anxiety was always difficult as I watched Nobby fighting for breath, helping him to suck the medication which might open his airways, or whatever it was supposed to do, as deep into his lungs as he could. I would find my own breathing begin to mirror his. Short, shallow, painful, desperate.

By the time I opened the bedroom door I was breathing hard from the run and the rush up the stairs. Nobby lay on his back, eyes wide, staring at the ceiling, his lips blue and his face white and I knew in that instant that my buddy, my best mate, my life friend and friend for life, Nobby Clark, was gone. The smog and the asthma had conspired to squeeze the last breath out of his lungs and refused to let him fill them up again.

I heard Julie behind me, and I turned. She leaned against the door frame, her hand to her mouth and we looked at each other, struggling to know what to say. I wanted to throw my head back, open my mouth and let go a howl. Vent the deepest grief I had ever felt, even greater than when my grandparents died. Dare I say, even than when my parents died. But I didn't. It had to remain inside, choked somewhere between my head, my heart and my throat. And there it would remain for ever, always on the very brink of escape.

I felt arms around me, and I became aware that time had begun again. I needed to lie down, collapse like a deflated balloon but I was being held up, or was it I who was holding someone up? I gradually returned to the here and now to find my arms tightly holding Julie to me. Her shoulders rose and fell, shook and heaved with her sobbing. Was it moments or days later that Mary's arms enfolded us both?

I have no recollection of the days leading to the funeral. Julie asked me to say something at the service, as Nobby's life-long friend, best man, family friend, substitute uncle to his kids. I got to my feet when I was invited but I could not tell if any words came out and, if they did, what they were. Mary said it was nice and Julie thanked me, but I have no idea what I said: how do you speak of your anger without sounding bitter, express regret at the future you won't share without sounding selfish, describe the deep importance of this person in your life, the love you felt, without raising curious eyebrows.

Mary was so patient with me for weeks. I knew I had to be quieter than I would normally be because that trapped howl of anguish might escape at the slightest provocation. I needed the children more intensely than ever to seal the gaping hole in my life but thinking of them did nothing but take me to the brink again. The walks to and from work were painful, silent trudges through the dark, frostiness of the encroaching winter. Lunch and tea breaks were solitary necessities: I had nothing to say to anyone and their chatter irritated me.

The letter from Mr and Mrs Davies came early in December and it punched a welcome hole in my gloomy cloud.

"Dear Mr and Mrs Robson

We wondered if you would be able to join us for Christmas. The children would love to have you here. They talk about you all the time and it would be nice for us to meet you.

You mustn't think of bringing anything with you – it's a bit easier for us in the country I think and on the farm we still have all we need for a good Christmas. But having you here would make it all the better.

Do please let us know you can come.

Yours, with very best wishes,

Brenda Davies"

Chapter 18

For most of the journey, which took best part of the day, I questioned in my mind the wisdom of what we were doing. The kindness of the Davieses inviting us to spend Christmas with them was undeniable and considerable, and it was that very fact that made me feel slightly uncomfortable. Mary assured me that they wouldn't have asked us if they hadn't wanted us to be there and spend a couple of days with the children but what could we offer in return? A couple of days in the smog? A short stay in the city with a chance of being bombed by Hitler? Hardly an attractive reciprocation.

And what could we bring as a contribution to the festivities? I was feeling increasingly uncomfortable about the things I had made for the Davies children – they were older than ours and I didn't know what might appeal to kids of their age. We had managed to get some dried fruit and Mary had made a Christmas cake, but we could bring little more.

The yellow and brown coach was parked outside the station as we emerged, suitcase in hand. Mary was genuinely excited about seeing the children and hurried towards the open door.

"Mary, we don't know if it's the right one."

"Don't be daft. I really don't think there'll be another, do you? And Mr Davies said it would be here when we arrived. Come on."

"We want to go to Valley Farm, please," Mary spoke to the driver.

"Oh, hello there. Brenda said you were coming. Come to spend Christmas with the kids eh? That's nice. That's sixpence for the two. You have a nice stay, won't you?"

There were three other people already on the bus who seemed to be eyeing us closely as we shuffled into the brown, velvet-upholstered seats. I turned to Mary: "How did he know who we were? How does he know Mrs Davies is called Brenda? He seems to know where the farm is."

"This isn't London, is it? I bet everyone knows everyone here. It's nice."

The bus climbed its way from the station and into the rolling countryside. The afternoon was cold, but the sky was clear and the air free from the choking fog we had come from. Even as dusk fell, from our elevated position in the bus we could see over the hedgerows either side of the narrow road, along which the bus rattled.

"I don't think I'll give the Davies children those things you know, Mary."

"You will," Mary replied firmly. "You spent ages making them and they'll love them."

"I wish we had more to bring to help with the Christmas dinner. And we should have got more for Mr and Mrs Davies. It's very kind of them to have us and I feel really awkward not bringing much."

"Will you give over. Mrs Davies said we were to bring nothing. She said we were very welcome, and she was looking forward to meeting us. Stop your worrying."

Maybe half an hour after we left the station the driver turned and called down the bus: "Valley Farm. Joe's just at the gate for you."

We exchanged Christmas greetings with the driver as we got off the bus and the man at the farm gate, dressed in heavy corduroy trousers, dark jacket, cap and boots stepped towards Mary with his hand outstretched.

"Joe Davies," he said. His face was ruddy and lined but I found it hard to decide his age: older than me but not of my parents' generation. He was thick-set and he filled his clothes easily – I doubt he could have buttoned his jacket over the thick woollen pullover beneath it. He was neither openly welcoming nor hostile: awkward perhaps. If it was that, then I shared his feeling.

"Hello, Mr Davies," Mary replied, shaking his hand. He turned to me and I put the case down, in order to take his hand. "Nice to meet you, Mr Davies," I said as our hands gripped each other's. "It's Joe," he said and reached with his free hand to pick the case up.

"It's fine," I said as I grabbed for the handle. Mary glared at me. "Thanks," I added.

Joseph strode out, untroubled by the puddles and ruts while Mary and I navigated the lane to the farmhouse as carefully as we could: we had with us only the shoes we were wearing, and we couldn't possibly walk mud into our hosts' house. Not another word was exchanged, and Joseph led the way past the front door, round the back of the house, to a door already open and all but filled by his wife who stood with her arms outstretched. She was wearing an apron and the warmest smile of greeting.

"Hello, my dears," she said, taking Mary into her open arms. "You must be so tired," she said as she released Mary and put her hand out for me to shake.

"It's so kind of you to invite us," Mary said.

"Where are the children? I thought they'd be here." I didn't mean to be rude and I wasn't ungrateful but that's all I had come for: to see my children and I really thought they'd be there to greet us. Surely, they missed me … us, as much as I … we, missed them.

"They don't know you're coming," Joe spoke for the first time since we left the station. "Brenda thought it would be the best surprise and in case something happened, and you couldn't make it. They'd have been disappointed."

With the broadest smile Brenda turned to her husband. "Excuse me, Mr Davies. It was *your* idea to keep it a surprise. I said we should tell them, and it was *you* who said it would be their best Christmas present!"

I'm sure I saw Joseph's face colour a little as he looked to the floor. In that moment I liked him so much more than when we first met. "It's been a nightmare making sure Bobby and Beckie kept the secret," Brenda added. "They're under instructions to keep Micky and Alice busy upstairs until we call them down."

"And our two are to stay up there until you've said your hellos," Joe explained.

Mary looked at me, took my hand and we smiled at each other.

"Would you like a cup of tea first or say hello to the children?" Brenda asked, knowing she needed no answer and Joseph had already walked to the bottom of the stairs.

Any anxiety I had ever had about how the children were cared for completely disappeared when I heard him call up the stairs. "Micky! Alice! Can you come down a minute? Got something I want you to see."

"In a minute, Mr D." It was Micky's voice calling back. "It's my turn."

"You might miss out," Joe called back, smiling and shaking his head gently.

"Coming."

I could hear a door open and Alice and Micky's voices, probably discussing why they might be wanted. Their footsteps came tumbling down the stairs and along the hallway towards the kitchen door. Unsurprisingly it was Micky who bowled in first with, "Yes, Mr D?" But as the words left him, he stopped dead in his tracks, his mouth open as Alice bundled into him from behind. Time froze for just a second and then exploded into a whirl of squeals and shrieks, hugs and kisses, jumps and skips.

Who knew who made the sounds and who cared: this was unadulterated joy for all four of us. We babbled our excitement, tripping over each other's words, tumbling over expressions of surprise, greeting, stories of our time apart, questions and declarations of love, all of which would have to be repeated to mean anything.

As we calmed a little, I turned to apologise to our hosts for our noise, but they weren't there. They had given their kitchen over to us to reassemble our family.

Chapter 19

Who could have believed just a few weeks ago that we would be spending Christmas Eve sat in a farmhouse sitting room with new-found friends, sharing our gazes between the roaring log fire and the decorated tree in the window bay? Micky sat on my lap, Alice beside Mary, Brenda and Joseph on what were clearly their designated chairs, Beckie was cross legged on the floor and Bobby sat leaning his back against the arm of his father's chair, legs stretched across the rug, the soles of his socked feet being warmed by the fire.

Micky had talked himself to exhaustion and was almost asleep. The two children had talked at both of us separately, simultaneously, trying to tell us of all the things they had been doing. It was Mr and Mrs D this, Bobby and Beckie that, a catalogue of learning and discovery, lambs being fed, eggs collected, falling in muck, herding of cows with Bobby, dressing dolls with Beckie, baking cakes with Mrs D and sharpening an axe with Mr D. I was envious. Envious of the place, of the life, envious of the children's relationship with their hosts.

"How's it been with Micky's bed?" Mary asked, with a knowing nod between mothers.

"Oh, nothing. We had a wet bed the first few nights, but Bobby sorted him. He was just the same at that age. Weren't you, Bob?"

"Mum! Please!"

"Oh, get on with you! Nothing since, have we, Micky?"

"No, Mrs D. Bobby wakes me up when he comes to bed, so I go to the lav."

"You know what?" It was Joseph who had spent much of the evening sitting quietly, drifting in and out of a doze, smiling occasionally at Micky's descriptions of the 'farming' he had done with Mr D. "I think we might drop the Mr and Mrs D. If it's all right with you Mr Robson I think Micky and Alice could call us Uncle Joe and Aunty Brenda."

Alice and Micky both looked at me to give permission for this level of familiarity, one which they previously enjoyed with Steve and Julie. It was that momentary recollection of Nobby's death and his widow's plight this Christmas that made my eyes fill. If Joseph interpreted it as gratitude for his gesture, then I didn't care too much.

"That's very kind of you, Joe."

"I'll put the kettle on the stove," said Joe and Brenda's gaze followed her husband's retreating back, mouth agape, not so much at his offer to the children but at him dealing with the kettle.

Chapter 20

Brenda had insisted that she and Joe would sleep in the front room and we were to have their bedroom. When we came down the next morning, she was busy at the stove and the enticing smell of cooking bacon filled the kitchen. Alice was laying the table and Beckie was slicing bread from a crusty cob loaf.

"Morning," Brenda called over her shoulder as she stirred porridge. "Sleep well?"

"Good thank you. Yes, really good." As I answered I realised just how well and deeply I *had* slept. I dreamt of a ten-year-old Nobby and me playing in the park and it was happy; I dreamt of holding tiny new-born Alice and I dreamt of Mary. London and the factory, smogs and sandbags, blackouts and barrage balloons seemed an age and a continent away. "Micky still in bed?"

"No!" Even her voice smiled. "He's with Bobby. They'll have got the cows in for Joe and gone to feed the chickens. Two less than yesterday!" She half turned to the plucked birds hanging on the back of the pantry door. I shrugged at Mary, sharing our disbelief at how our two wonderful children had endeared themselves so much to these kind people. I felt pumped full of parental pride.

Breakfast done we all went to the sitting room where the fire had been rekindled from the night before and blazed on. A little pile of neatly wrapped gifts waited below the tree. Mary had brought a tin of biscuits and it seemed totally inadequate and I was so unsure of my gifts to the Davies children. We'd done our best for Micky and Alice in terms of presents but we couldn't carry much, and they showed just the right pleasure when they opened them later – in fact, they both seemed less interested in their gifts this year and kept saying how pleased they were to see us.

Micky opened one last present from Joe and Brenda and found a pair of green Wellington boots. I think they'd been Bobby's before, but Micky would have loved them even more had he known. Alice had a wrap-round apron which Brenda had shortened for her. Two last presents remained, mine to Bobby and Beckie. Beckie at least pretended to like the ballet dancer I'd carved from a piece of wood. It had taken hours and hours to get it delicate and slim, shiny-smooth and polished. She showed it to her mother and father and said she loved it. By the way she held on to it, looking at it and stroking her hand over the figure I think she might genuinely have been pleased with her gift. "Did you really make it, Mr Robson?" she asked more than once.

Bobby had seemed only vaguely pleased with the gifts of socks and a new shirt from his parents, so I expected a less enthusiastic reaction from him. I told him to unwrap his carefully and when he finally peeled off all the newspaper I'd used as padding he held my gift in the palms of his two hands. "Look, Dad." He presented the gift to his father like the three kings do at every school nativity play. I was pleased with the way the blade I had honed shone, it's edge fine and sharp. The wooden handle I had attached was smoothly shaped for the perfect hold.

"It's amazing, Mr Robson. I love it, just love it. And you really made this, too?"

"Yes."

"Is it okay for me to have it, Dad?" the boy remembered to ask.

"Of course it is, Bobby. Just treat it properly and be really careful."

"I will. It's the best. Just amazing. Thank you."

This was the best Christmas ever. Just my mate Nobby was missing to make it perfect.

Chapter 21

If the mighty oak table which dominated the kitchen could have groaned it surely would as the Christmas dinner was spread across it. Bowls of steaming vegetables formed a line down the centre and Brenda tried not to make too much of a grand gesture as she carried the golden-roasted chickens from the oven and placed them proudly in front of her husband.

Christmas dinner was devoured with a brandy-flamed pudding providing a perfect and spectacular finale which had the children cheering and clapping – even Bobby forgot his age and joined in unashamedly.

"Thank you." I didn't know I was going to say aloud what I was thinking, and it took me, as well as everyone else, by surprise when the words came out in a rare moment of quiet as the pudding was being eaten.

"You're all very welcome," Joe replied. He meant it and I felt it.

The day was one of candles, flaming fires, laughter, too much food, friendship which I never expected and a family closeness I feared I might never experience again when I said goodbye to our little ones three months earlier. I knew they were safe and cared for and that made me feel both relieved and envious. The chatter hardly stopped, even for the parlour games during which everyone accused everyone else of cheating and loving it all the more for that.

Micky and Alice promised to show us the farm the next day, the fast-growing calves and lambs, the hay loft, the tractor and, after checking it was all right with newly appointed Uncle Joe, we were promised to be allowed to collect the eggs from the chicken run. More than once I caught Bobby looking at his knife and he even showed his dad some feature or other he particularly liked. Beckie had her dancer in the lap of her dress all the time she sat on the floor.

When it was time for the children to go to bed, later than normal for ours because it was Christmas Day, it was Bobby and Beckie who took the lead and supervised our two. "Piggyback, Bobby," was about all a sleepy Micky could manage from the place on my lap he had occupied for the last hour or so of the evening. Bobby nodded, turned and knelt in front of me so that I could lift Micky onto his back. Micky wrapped his arms around my neck just a little tighter, kissed my cheek and said, "Night, night, Daddy."

"Night night, Soldier." And, in a whisper I added, "I love you."

"Love you too. All round the world and back again twice."

"Night all," said Bobby. "And thanks again for my knife, Mr Robson."

Alice scooted round the room giving everyone a good night kiss, thanking each one for a lovely day and declaring it was her 'best Christmas ever.' Hand in hand with Beckie she disappeared to bed.

The fire was beginning to quiet and was now little more than grey-red embers. I wanted to throw more logs onto it to keep it roaring and lengthen the day. For ever.

Mary and Brenda began a gentle chatter, recapping the successes of the day's food, how all the presents had been perfect and both praising each other's children for their good behaviour and manners when they were each bursting with pride that their own offspring had done them proud.

Chapter 22

Joseph turned his gaze from the glowing fireplace to me. We had exchanged few words all day: indeed, I suspected he might be a man of few words and probably didn't share the sort of bond with another man that I enjoyed with Nobby. *Had* enjoyed with Nobby.

"How is it?" he asked.

I hesitated. I welcomed the conversation and answered quickly, enthusiastically, to let him know. But I wasn't sure what I was being asked.

"Sorry Mr … Joe. How's …?" I stumbled.

"How's things, in London. With the war, and that?"

"You know what? Nothing! We're all prepared, what with sandbags and blackouts, but nothing. Makes you wonder why we sent the kids away. They keep telling us on the radio that it'll come soon but who knows when? We've got our coupons for the rationing they say will have to start in the new year. Fuel's not easy to come by already."

"That'd be a problem here. Don't know how I'd do without the tractor. I don't have a horse that could do the work anymore. I guess farms and the like will be protected somehow." He paused. "You work in the munitions factory, Micky was telling me."

"Yes. You wouldn't believe how the work has got. The stockpiles are like mountains. I tell you what, if one of them went up half of London would disappear, I reckon, and Jerry wouldn't have had to do a thing!"

Joe blew his cheeks out and I reflected on what I'd just said. It was probably true, and I hadn't thought it before I said it.

"What's that, love? London disappearing?" Mary joined the conversation.

I didn't repeat what I'd said. "We must let these people go to bed, Mary. They're up at the crack of dawn." And that was it: the end of a day the like of which I had neither wanted or expected but which I had enjoyed more than I could ever have hoped or imagined. We said our good nights and within minutes we were snuggled under the layers of blankets Brenda had supplied for their bed she insisted we use for our stay.

"What a lovely day," whispered Mary. "Aren't they nice people?"

"We were very lucky. Hope Nobby and Julie's kids have done as well."

There was a pause.

"You miss Nobby."

I could only nod my head, unseen in the dark, kiss Mary goodnight and turn away to try and sleep.

Chapter 23

The Boxing Day tour of the farm was a whirl of cows, sheep, chickens, cats, dogs, manure, tractor riding, children handholding, lifting and swinging. And boot retrieving. Bobby's passed-on boots were just a little too large for Micky, but he cared not a jot, even when one filled with slurry after a spectacular launch from his foot when I swung him high in the air. The event reduced everyone to laughter which became uncontrolled when Micky shoved his foot back into it and muck shot over the top and up his leg.

"Hey, they're my best boots you've got on!" Bobby declared through his laughter. "And now you've filled them with cow shit!"

Brenda cuffed Bobby round the back of the head and, just at the moment the hysterics were subsiding, his 'shit' and Brenda's hit set us all off again. But worse. Alice declared she was going to wet herself. Brenda and Mary held onto each other as if they were weakened by the laughter and might stumble to the floor and I put my hands on my knees and blew my cheeks out to try and regain some sort of composure. When Bobby took his boots and socks off, rolled the bottoms of his trousers up and began to plodge barefoot through the yard slurry towards the backdoor, as if to walk straight in, Brenda screeched, "Don't you dare!" Of course, he wouldn't but the whole idea set off another wave of puerile giggling.

Once back indoors turns were taken by the boys to wash their feet in the bathtub, Micky needing just a little more washing than that as the muck had squirted up his legs. I was sent into the front room to supervise – Bobby would have to take his trousers off so Mary knew she would not be welcome, and I would have to deal with Micky. It was another moment of closeness with my boy that I wanted to take away with me when we left later that afternoon.

"Will you make me a knife?" Micky asked.

"When you're as big as Bobby I will. You will keep it safe won't you, Bobby?"

"Yes, Mr Robson. 'Course I will."

Both boys washed, dried and dressed we joined the women in the kitchen and ate some cold meat, bread, cheese and slices of the Christmas cake Mary had made, all washed down with seemingly endless cups of tea. Brenda claimed she had never tasted a cake so good and Mary dismissed the compliment with a wave of her hand, but I knew she was pleased.

Too soon the time came for Joe to take us to the station for our train home. Goodbyes were sad but not despairing as they had been when we saw the children off from home. Now we knew where they were: they were being cared for better than we could have dared hope for. And they were happy. I would miss them no less, but I would no longer worry about them. Just envy them.

Beckie hugged Mary and waved to me. Bobby shook both our hands and thanked me yet again for the knife. Brenda hugged us both and then shepherded her two out of the kitchen and left us with our kids. We said our goodbyes but there were no tears: long, tight hugs and declarations of love, but no tears. Mary held hers back until we were in the Bedford van heading for the station.

Joe kissed Mary on the cheek and then took my hand. Just as I was about to let it go, he wrapped his other hand around mine and said, "Take care. Remember you're always welcome to come and visit. Don't worry about the kids, we'll take good care of them."

"I know. Thank you, Joe. Thank you so much."

Chapter 24

Having talked until we slept on the train into Euston, we travelled the tube and walked from the bus stop to the house in silence. The Underground walls were covered with warning and guidance posters: we'd been told that the tube stations would be used as shelters in the event of bombing and the signs shattered any of the residual peace we felt from the farm.

This was *our* reality, a world away from that of the Davieses. The cold there was crisp and clean, fresh and invigorating, the air pure and energising. Instead, as we stepped out of the Underground, I felt a thick, penetrating dampness, the invisible filth in each breath almost immediately began to coat my lungs. I didn't want to be here. I didn't want to make my now solitary walk to the factory the next day. In that moment I hated London, I hated the munitions factory and I hated, with a vengeance, the scrawny, jumped up German who had separated me from my children. And, just for a split second I was angry with Nobby for leaving me to deal with this on my own.

I felt Mary take my hand and I remembered I was not on my own at all.

There was nothing to celebrate on New Year's Eve so we didn't. Mary said I should check on Elsie over the road. "Take a bit of coal and do first footing. Wish her a happy New Year."

"You are joking, Mary. What sort of new year has she got to look forward to?"

The days fell back into the routine we had established before Christmas: Mary cleaning, lengthening days for me at the factory, evenings by the fire listening to the latest developments of Hitler's advances in Poland and his ambitions for France. Occasional letters from the children continued in the same vein, full of happiness and contentment and the need to have them return grew and grew. I could not recognise it at the time, but I began to fear I might never fully get them back. Even when they returned would they always hanker to be back on the farm? How strong would their affections for the Davieses become?

Jealousy is a destructive thing and it was growing inside me: I was jealous of the life my children were enjoying and I was jealous of the fact that it was Joe and Brenda who were seeing them enjoy it, not me. I knew it was happening, but I couldn't stop myself from becoming quieter. Conversations at work stopped: I had nothing in common with the few men still working and the women grouped themselves at breaks to chatter and gossip about whatever women do.

I felt intensely alone at work and at home Mary and I seemed not to be drifting apart but to be less intensely connected. I loved her no less and needed her more than ever but the growing turbulence in my head was somehow melting the glue that bound us together.

It was made worse when, one night, Mary snuggled close to me in bed and kissed me in the way I knew was not just goodnight. I wrapped my arms around her and felt her hand reach into my pyjama trousers and take gentle hold of me. I kissed her and slid my hand inside her nightie and felt the wonderful, soft warmth of her breast. She deftly untied the cord of my pyjamas and used her foot to push them down, all the while fondling me as she pressed her tongue past my lips.

I felt loved and safe and wanted. In return I loved Mary, I would keep her safe *and* I wanted her, too. So very much. But my body was not telling her that. Much as I wanted to, no matter how much I was trying to react as I would normally do in an instant, even without the perfect stimulation Mary was providing, nothing was happening. She became more urgent, whispering things in my ear designed to arouse me and I wanted desperately for my body to show I wanted this.

I tried to fill my head with recollections of our passionate, abandoned lovemaking before the children. I recalled times of whispered passion and stifled climaxes when the children were in the next room. I even tried to think of Mary and I engaged in things some of the men at work claimed to indulge in with their wives and girlfriends: whilst I doubted most of it, the talk would sometimes cause me to have to hide my reaction. But when I came back to Mary, beside me right then and there, I was acutely aware that I had not reacted much at all. Neither her attention nor my imaginings had made me ready and Mary withdrew her hand.

"I'm sorry." I turned my back to her and drew my knees up towards my chest.

Behind me Mary moulded her body to mine, wrapped her arms around me and whispered in my ear, "I love you."

"I love you too. Always."

I stared into the thick blackness. I was twenty-nine for God's sake. For more than fifteen years I had hardened at a mere thought, had ignored the myths of madness and blindness and pleasured myself at will until Mary and I married, and sometimes even after. I was a man in his prime, not some wilting fifty odd year old, a man with a lovely, loving wife who never denied my pleasure, sometimes even letting me know the pleasure she felt too. We had the house to ourselves, no fitfully sleeping children to disturb. But I couldn't do it.

I wouldn't even be able to seek reassurance in some cautious, tip-toeing talk with Nobby. He'd have teased me mercilessly once I confessed to what happened, think up all sorts of cruel jibes: I'd have looked across to his workplace and he'd put his finger in the air and allow it to droop. And then, perhaps, he'd admit it had happened to him. Not to worry. It's all that's going on, he'd reassure me. Happens to the best of us. Every now and then. And then it would be just occasional teasing until, over a pint, he'd ask how things were. You know, in the bedroom department. And I'd tell him it was all fine. Just a one-off. That's the ticket, he'd say. And then there'd be no more mention.

Just like when his rabbit died when he was ten or so. I popped round to play and he was in the yard, his rabbit cradled in his arms. Nobby was crying. Of course, we'd both cried when we'd fallen over and scraped our knees but that was pain. This was grief. "Lucky's dead," he said without looking up. At the time, I didn't realise the deep irony of the poor rabbit's name, just crouched beside him and put my arm across his shoulder.

He cried a bit more when we buried the floppy, furry animal. We dug a hole so deep and the registry office door opened, and we walked in and they both said "I do" while I held out the ring.

"Please raise your glasses and toast the bride and groom. To Nobby, I mean Steve, and Julie Clarke." We danced till we dropped and stumbled home, Mary steadying me in my tipsy state as we giggled our way up the stairs. "Where have you been?" Alice quizzed us from her bedroom door. A sheep bleated from outside and I looked through the window to see Nobby, or was it Micky, looking up at me, just as the whole thing exploded in a deafening flash. Clods of earth, bricks and limbs flew into the air, amid billowing smoke and Mary's face appeared from within it, like an angel. She was smiling, calling my name and telling me to wake up. Wake up.

"Wake up! Wake up!"

I sat up, eyes wide, wide open, searching for something to tell me where I was. It was Mary's eyes I found. "Wake up," she said. "You're all right, my sweet." And she put her arms around me.

Chapter 25

Winter on the farm was harsh. The novelty for the visiting children wore off and they began to miss home. Bobby and Beckie tried to remain patient but Alice's fussiness became irritating and Micky's unceasing energy and curiosity began to niggle Bobby, who increasingly craved time and space to himself.

Joe's neck seemed to shrink further into his jacket collar as the days came cold and wet, one after the other, and Brenda alone seemed able to sail her way unerringly through each day, whatever the moods of those around her.

Joe always found this January February time, the very dead of winter, the hardest to deal with. Every chore, each routine action hurt with cold. His woollen gloves quickly became sodden and oft times they crunched with icy cold as he clenched his fingers around a handle, a post, a gate. Any time outside was bearable only with the knowledge that he could thaw out by the stove in an hour or two. He would drape his soaking gloves on the range, his jacket on the back of a chair as close to the heat as he dare, and watch the steam rise from them, all but praying that they would be dry and warm by the time he had to put them on again.

"I need your help putting some hay out later, Bobby."

"Oh, Dad. Do I have to?"

"Bob!" Brenda intervened before Joe had a chance to react to his son's reluctance. "You help your dad, love. It won't take the two of you long. You could use your knife on the twine perhaps. That's right isn't it, Joe? He could cut the twine with it."

"I've got a knife of my …"

"Joe! Bobby's knife would be useful, and he hasn't got to use it properly yet." Brenda had become expert at negotiating the minefield between her husband and his son. She could see how similar they were when they could not.

"We'll go out after I've drunk me tea," was the only reply.

"Can I come too?" Micky asked, oblivious to the unresolved tension which still hung in the air.

Brenda replied without checking with her husband. "If you want, Pet. But you'll have to wrap up warm and not get in the way." In an instant the boy had scuttled off to put on as many layers as he could find and soon presented himself fully prepared, apart from coat, boots and the multi-coloured gloves Brenda had knitted him from wool ends she had.

"Come on then, Bob. I think the boss is ready," Joe said more good-humouredly and the next few minutes were a bustle of coat, glove, hat and boot fitting. As the door opened a freezing blast of iced air forced itself into the room, instantly consuming the heat and causing Brenda to gasp.

The three dropped their heads against the razor-like wind and headed across the yard for the barn, negotiating the frozen ruts and puddles. It made little difference when they closed the barn door behind them: the cold sliced through every gap it could find in the building and would take time to warm.

"We'll need half a dozen bales, Bobby," Joe instructed as he looked at the stack before them. Micky was already tugging ineffectually at the twine around one of the bales at the base of what, to him, was nothing less than a hay mountain.

"Not them, Micky. We need the dry ones from the top," Bobby explained, smiling at Micky's belief that he could budge any of them. "You want me to go up, Dad?" he asked his father.

"If you like. Take your time and be sure of your footing."

"Dad! I *have* done it before."

"I know that lad. I'm just reminding you. Doesn't hurt to remind, does it?"

Bobby began to clamber up the accidentally created steps of the haystack which rocked slightly each time he climbed to the next level. Micky stared upwards with both awe and envy. He had come to idolise his new mentor and to see him managing this perilous and exciting accent was thrilling and made him admire him still more.

"Whoah!" Bobby shouted as he feigned a wobble, a potential fall.

"That's enough," Joe insisted. "No more messing Bobby: you're a fair way up now. You'll give yourself more than a headache if you come down from there, that's for sure. Go for the one on your left first and that will give you a firm footing for the rest. Just make sure you're steady, okay."

Bobby used the binding twine to pull himself a little further up and spied the bale his father was recommending. "This one?" he checked.

"Yeah. Check it's not snagged on the ones either side."

"Got it. Seems good, Dad. Ready below?"

"Micky, go and stand over there, well out of the way."

Micky backed off, still staring up at his hero above.

"Go!" Joe called and seconds later a spiky yellow box began to float through the air, seemingly getting bigger as it plummeted, tumbling towards the barn floor. As it landed there was mighty thud and it looked as though it might explode with the impact. It bounced a little, a cloud of golden dust-sparks rising from it, up and out, still settling long after the bale had come to rest.

Joe couldn't help but smile as he turned to see Micky, open-mouthed and clapping at the spectacle he had just witnessed. The boy rushed forward to get as close as he could to wonder how the bale had remained largely intact even after its awesome fall. He flapped his arms to waft away the dust, coughed and spluttered.

Neither he nor Joe was aware of the second bale which had dislodged itself and was following the first towards the ground.

"Micky!" shrieked Bobby and Micky was delighted that Bobby was just as excited as he was.

Chapter 26

London winter is always cold, grey, dank but the ominous threat of war made it all the more so. At home, warmth could only be found within a few feet of the fire blazing in the sitting room hearth and even that felt one-sided. The air on the side away from the fire remained stubbornly cold. That was about the only saving grace being at the factory: I reckoned I could be warm for much of the day as I worked near the forge belching out its heat as the glowing, molten metal slithered into the moulds.

Chat was never easy over the din of the machines, the clanging and grinding drowning out all but the loudest shouts. But in the winter months, even break times were quieter than in the summer. I found I had nothing to say to anyone. Head down I got on with my work – in fact, the foreman actually praised me for the rate I was turning out finished products and I was now used to check on the others, to make sure the quality was consistent. "We can't have the bloody things blowing up before they reach Jerry, can we?"

The days and evenings lacked the lightness that the children brought. The absence of their babbling voices, their shrieks and giggles, even their bickering, made life seem mundane, a drudge, dull, lifeless. More frightening than anything was that life like this started to feel like normal: this is as it is. And I didn't want that.

The mood in London, perhaps in the whole country but who knew, was depressed: we were stuck in a cold, wet, stagnant ditch of frightened expectation. Rationing had started as they said it would, the sandbags and sticky tape were in place, the underground stations were set up and some people had even constructed shelters in their gardens. For what? There was still no sign of the threatened bombs and Mary and I began to talk about bringing the children home.

It was our choice, after all, and why not get them back? There was no compulsion to keep them away and, after more than six months during which nothing had happened to vindicate our decision to send them away, it began to feel cruel to both them and us to remain separated.

I wrestled with it all in my thoughts almost constantly, weighing up the tug of the heart with that of the head: they were safe where they were, cared for and living a life which, even from our short visit, I had come to envy. Regardless of the imminent threat to the city, it was hard to find fault with living in clean air, at one with the rhythm, smells and colours of nature. It had to be better for our children: safe and worry-free.

As Mary and I ate our increasingly meagre and uninteresting evening meals, cleared the dishes and sat by the fire listening to the wireless, we would mull over the options time and again. Talking about the children no longer reduced Mary to tears immediately, though particular recollections might. I just ached inside, permanently. For all I knew Mary may have been feeling that very same pain, but I didn't say how I was feeling, and I didn't ask her. I couldn't. I just clung to an image of our two kids discovering a different way of life, happy and secure, but hoping they weren't enjoying it too much.

"If nothing's happened by the end of the month, let's get them home," Mary broke the silence one evening.

"Do what?"

"I said, if nothing's happened, no bombs, no warnings by the end of this month, let's get the kids back. They can always go away again if needs be."

"But we know they're safe there."

"No safer than here really. At least not for the time being. They've been telling us for the last six months that Hitler's going to bomb us any day soon and still nothing. I think it was all an excuse. Make the rations stretch further."

"I don't think that, Mary, but it would be nice to have them back. What are you saying? That we wait till the end of Feb and then decide?"

Chapter 27

The bale left the top of the stack and tumbled downwards. Joe looked up at Bobby's cry and then to Micky who was now directly under its line of decent. Who knew why Micky looked up? Perhaps some sense that the air above him was changing. Maybe there was some sound as the hay bale shifted within its twine as it fell but Joe saw the look on the boy's face the second before the bale struck him.

Was it a look of shock or puzzlement? Did he, in that moment, have any idea of the weight of the bale or the power of such a weight falling from a height? He could have no idea of the possible consequences, that was for certain.

In that very same second Joe was wondering how he would tell the boy's Mum and Dad. He should never have let the boy into the barn while he and his son worked? He told Brenda the farm wasn't safe for these city children. He said they couldn't manage two. He lunged towards the boy just as the bale completed its fall.

Micky had instinctively dropped his head just before the bale landed, so it struck him across the shoulders. As the monstrous weight crushed him to the barn floor, he made no sound: even the sound of the air inside him being forced out by the impact was drowned by the sickening thud of the bale landing.

For a second time, dust billowed out and the dry hay made a crackling sound as it strained to break out of its bindings. It twisted and buckled but when it settled it had retained its neat box shape.

Bobby was already scrambling down the stack shouting Micky's name. And then, "Dad! Dad! Quick!" Joe was sprawled on the barn floor, pushed aside without realising it by the bale, even as the consequences of this were still forming themselves in his mind.

When he reached the ground Bobby could see only the lower half of Micky's legs protruding from beneath the bale. He may have been imagining it, but they seemed to lie awkwardly and not as they should be. He started to tug at the twine to shift the bale off the boy, but he couldn't budge it alone. "Dad!" he yelled and grabbed the knife that Micky's dad had given him from the sheath inside his sock.

He slashed the twine with the knife and began to tear the hay away. "Dad!" he shouted again and, at last, Joe stirred and joined his son to grab at handfuls of hay. As he was frantically pulling at it, Joe realised that, had the twine still been in place, he could have lifted the bale away in one heave.

"Bobby, you've cut the twine, you idiot. I can't lift it now!

"Just get it out the way, Dad. We've nearly cleared it."

Soon Micky's whole body was exposed, looking for all the world like a sleeping animal, cossetted and cushioned by the hay. He was still, no sign of injury other than the slightly unnatural angles at which his arms and legs rested. Only that and the lack of sound or movement, something never true of Micky unless he was asleep, suggested anything might be amiss.

Joe was functioning again. "Don't move him, Bob." He knelt beside Micky and, whilst very gently resting one hand on the boy's back, he used his other to steady himself as he leaned down and placed his ear beside the boy's mouth.

"Micky!" Bobby called.

"Shhh!" his father snapped, and he moved still closer, until his ear pressed against the boy's cheek. He could just feel a rise and fall under his hand and a wisp of air escaping from between the boy's slightly parted lips brushed onto his face.

"He's alive, Bobby. Go and get your mum and then you cycle to the village and get Mrs Jenkins to phone for the doctor." It was Bobby's turn to freeze: his face was ashen and he had seemingly regressed several years in an instant and needed his father to insist before he got to his feet.

"Now, Bobby! Now!"

The boy turned tail and ran to the barn door, forcing himself through the gap without waiting for it to swing comfortably wide. He ran full pelt across the frozen yard.

"Mum! Mum!" he yelled even before he had reached the kitchen door. "Mum, it's Micky. Dad needs you in the barn. It's Micky!"

"Dear God, Bob. What's happened?"

"A bale fell on him. Dad's with him. I've got to go to the village. To get the doctor. He's not moving, Mum." He didn't know it, but he was crying: it was the feel of wetness that made him wipe the sleeve of his jacket across his eyes and his nose. He ran back out of the door and across to the shed where his bike was. Ignoring that the tyres needed to be pumped up, he leapt over the cross bar and, without sitting on the saddle, began to pedal furiously across the yard. He bumped, rattled and skidded over the ruts and tracks in the frozen mud and through the gate to the lane.

Brenda threw her coat over her apron and grabbed a quilt that was folded across the arm of the chair by the range. She slipped her feet into her boots and made her way to the barn in a strange walk-come-run which would have been comical had it not been for the reason for her haste.

She found her husband crouched over a small mound in the hay strewn across the barn floor. His arm rested across the boy's back and he was whispering into his ear, though Brenda could not hear what. When she spoke Joe either did not hear or he ignored her, so she moved closer, opening the quilt.

"Joe, let's keep him warm," she said. "Joe."

At last, her husband looked up, said nothing but moved his arm away to allow the quilt to be laid over the boy. As soon as it was in place Joe returned his hand and went back to whispering into Micky's ear.

"'s all right, you'll be fine, little fella. Bobby's gone for the doctor and they'll be here soon. Don't you worry. Uncle Joe's here to look after you."

Unable to offer anything more, Brenda simply put her hand on Joe's shoulder and left him to reassure the still motionless boy.

Chapter 28

The decision was made. Mary and I agreed that there was no reason for the children not to come home and I felt absurdly elated. Perhaps I hadn't realised just how deeply the sadness of their absence had affected me: I knew I didn't like it; I knew I missed them, and I was unhappy; I knew I had become increasingly uncommunicative and irritable but the decision to bring them home had an immediate and noticeable effect. "What are you smiling at?" Mary asked as we washed the dishes.

"Was I?"

"Yes, you were. And I can guess but I want to hear you say it," Mary teased.

"I can't wait to see them. It will be so good to have them home again. We should never have sent them away, Mary."

"Don't be daft. We did what we were told was best and they've had a wonderful time, you know. They've learnt a lot and, if anything had kicked off, we knew they were safe and sound. We were so lucky that the Davieses took them in. They've been so kind to them, and Micky's quite taken to Bobby."

"I'm going to write to them once we've cleared away. Explain what we're thinking," I said to Mary as I put the last of the pots into the cupboard. "I don't want them to think we're unhappy with anything or ungrateful."

I sat at the table instead of the chair by the fire. I'd been rehearsing in my head what I might say in the letter and I began to write.

"Dear Joe and Brenda"

"Do you think it's all right to call them Joe and Brenda, or should I say Mr and Mrs Davies?" I asked Mary.

"Joe and Brenda's fine. They said so."

"Dear Joe and Brenda

We cannot thank you enough for looking after Alice and Micky for the last few months. You have been so kind to them and we know they have become very fond of you all.

As you know nothings happened here and the Germans show no signs of dropping there bombs on us. Lots of children have come back to London and we think we should take our two off your hands. We know there happy and safe with you but we do miss them very much and would like them to come home.

What we have decided is to wait a couple more weeks and if nothings happening we will be in touch again to make arrangements for one of us to come and collect them.

We think it's probably best if you dont say anything to the children until nearer the time, just in case plans have to change. Mickys a handfull enough without having him excited about coming home!

Very best wishes

Tom and Mary Robson"

I read the letter to Mary to get her approval and said. "I'll put that in the post on my way to work in the morning."

Chapter 29

It felt to Bobby like an age for him to reach Mrs Jenkins'. He pummelled on the door until she opened it and gave her no time to protest at the noise. "Mrs Jenkins, please phone the doctor. Micky's in the barn. A bale hit him. He's hurt really bad. Please hurry. I think his legs are broke. Dad's with him. It fell so far."

The habitually brusque woman could see the distress in the boy's face and scooped an arm round his shoulder.

"Come in, Bobby. Calm down and tell me what's happened while I phone Dr Garrett." The telephone sat grandly on a stand in the hallway and Mrs Jenkins lifted the receiver, keeping her gaze on Bobby as she waited for the operator to answer.

"Hello, Ella. Can you put me through to Dr Garrett, please? As fast as you can." She smiled at Bobby to reassure him that things would soon be in hand but even she became impatient at the wait.

"Oh, hello, Doctor, there's been an accident at the Davieses' farm. The evacuee. Seems a bale fell on him…I don't know. Just a moment: the Davies boy is here, I'll ask him." Unnecessarily she covered the mouthpiece with her hand. "Is he conscious Bobby?"

"No. Dad said he was breathing but said not to move him, but he wasn't moving. He wasn't saying anything. He didn't cry or anything. He was just lying…"

She removed her hand. "No, Doctor. Seems he was unconscious… Right…Yes…I'll send Bobby back there with that message. Thank you, Doctor."

Mrs Jenkins rested the telephone back on its cradle and placed a hand on each of Bobby's arms and looked directly into his moistened eyes, mostly to be sure of having his full attention and, though she would deny it, to reassure him.

"Dr Garrett is on his way. You go straight back and tell your Mum and Dad to keep him warm, not to move him, keep him as calm as they can. Go on, off you go."

Bobby half smiled, turned, went back out of the still open front door, remounted his bike and headed back for the farm. As he pedalled, it occurred to him that he would be back home only shortly before the doctor arrived, so he redoubled his effort. Head down, leaning over the handlebars, he hurtled down the lane.

While Bobby headed home, Mrs Jenkins donned her coat and hat and headed for Miss Hastings' house. Though her billeting officer duties were finished it occurred to Mrs Jenkins that the little boy's parents might need to be told and the person who distributed the evacuees in the first place was probably best placed to know where they came from.

Meanwhile Dr Garrett had grabbed his Gladstone bag, some splints, extra bandages and vials of morphine. He put his hat and coat on one handed as he walked to the Morris 8 which, thankfully, despite the cold and damp, started first time.

He knew the Davies family as well as he knew most of the folk who lived in the three villages he served: he had delivered Bobby and Rebecca; he had bandaged and treated Joe a couple of times for minor injuries; treated Brenda for the common post-partum complaints. All the normal things a family doctor was called on to tend. As he drove, however, he had an ominous feeling that this was serious, perhaps beyond the care he could administer and, most importantly, probably beyond the family's means. A bale of hay weighed a lot and one falling on a little boy was bad. Really bad.

Chapter 30

Joe maintained his vigil at Micky's side. He was not a religious man, but he found himself thinking some sort of prayer in his head. Was it just a hope, a wish or was he thinking that only if there was a God could Micky survive? If, by chance, there was one then he'd best ask as best he could for the little lad to recover.

Brenda had been back to the house and brought a hot, sweet tea for her husband, but it remained untouched on the barn floor. She had seen him gentle and quite demonstrative with their own children when they were small but there had never been a time when either had been in this sort of peril and the big man could not have looked more gentle, or more caring than he did at that moment. Nor as vulnerable and worried.

She felt strangely useless in what was, after all, a domestic situation involving a child, albeit not their own, which she would usually think of as her domain. But Joe was there, beside the boy, still whispering reassurance in his ear.

It was she who heard Bobby's bike crash onto the yard ground, and she hurried to the barn door to get news of the doctor and to tell her boy to go in quietly for fear of startling either Joe or Micky, should he come round.

"Is he all right?" Bobby asked.

"Your Dad's with him. He's awake now, I think. He'll be fine, I'm sure, Bobby. Go in quietly, now." She knew she could not, and should not, keep him out.

Bobby eased sideways through the part open barn door and almost tiptoed towards his dad and the still prostrate boy. He put his hand on his father's shoulder and almost whispered, "The Doctor's on his way, Dad."

Joe took his hand from Micky's back for the first time since he placed it there and put it onto Bobby's as it rested on his shoulder, squeezed it very slightly and said, "Good lad. Good lad."

And that was the scene that Doctor Garrett found when Brenda led him into the barn once he had pulled the car to a halt and grabbed his bag from the passenger seat.

Bobby turned and, seeing the doctor, felt a wave of relief.

"Dad, the doctor's here." But Joe didn't move. "Dad," he repeated. He moved aside as Doctor Garrett reached them but still Joe made no move and the doctor placed a hand on each of the crouching man's arms and said, "Come on, Joe, let me see the little fella."

At last he stood and caught Bobby's gaze. His son saw his father's eyes red and moist, tear-streaks down each side of the big man's face and he simply walked to him and wrapped his arms round him. Joe wiped his sleeve across his eyes.

"It's all the bloody dust," Joe said.

"I know," Bobby replied. "'S awful."

The doctor was kneeling beside Micky, holding his wrist and counting silently as he looked at his pocket watch. Then he moved the blanket away and ran his hands down each arm and then each leg. Without looking up or pausing his examination he said,

"How long has he been here, Joe?"

"I'm not sure, Doc. Half an hour, an hour maybe."

"Has he said anything?"

"Nothing really, Doc. Just mutterings and groans. Is he going to be all right?"

"I think he might have broken his leg but I'm more concerned that he's been out for such a long time. Might be unconscious, might be shock. His pulse is good. His breathing is regular."

"He looks like he's asleep," said Bobby. "He looks like that when I go up to bed. He's always out like a light when I go up and he sleeps on his front. I think he's just asleep. I bet that's it.

"He needs to go to the hospital, Joe."

"But I don't have the money for an ambulance and all that, Doc."

"My surgery would be next best but let's at least get him inside and be sure he's warm. We need to make a stretcher of some sort: I don't want to carry him in case he *has* broken something."

Without any bidding Bobby was away. He found two fence posts he knew were standing in the corner of the barn and some spare twine from the bailing. He found his knife lying on the barn floor and busied himself cutting lengths of the twine and then slicing holes in the quilt that had been over Micky. Joe cottoned on to what his son was constructing and joined in while the doctor removed his coat and used it to replace the quilt over Micky.

The make-shift stretcher made, Joe and the doctor carefully lifted the boy onto it. He made a sound. A pained groan. The two men paused. Joe looked at the doctor who made a face which suggested that this was a good sign, an almost imperceptible nod and a downturned smile.

Bobby heard the sound too, turned and ran ahead, bursting through the back door. "Mum, they're bringing him inside. He made a noise."

Beckie was occupying Alice at the kitchen table. Alice had been upstairs when the whole thing began but she had been asking where her brother was and why Bobby had gone off on his bike and who the man in the car was and, again, where Micky was. Between them, Brenda and Beckie had avoided her questions and reassured her that the 'men' were busy on farm things. But Bobby's latest entry ignited the fears she had been harbouring that something was wrong.

"Who are they bringing in?" she asked.

"Why don't you two girls go upstairs for a bit, just while the men get sorted," Brenda suggested.

"Where's Micky?" Alice demanded.

Brenda knew she couldn't keep the secret much longer and Joe and the doctor must be on their way across the yard. "Micky had a fall in the barn, Pet. The doctor's come to check he's okay. They're bringing him inside, in the warm. Would you take the cushions off the sofa for me and then we can put him on there? He'll be comfy on that, near the fire. Beckie, would you get another blanket from the cupboard for me and I'll make some tea."

With everyone busily occupied anyone would have thought it was a normal evening in the Davies farmhouse until the two men came through the door, carrying Micky, now on his back, on the makeshift stretcher. They crossed the flag stone kitchen floor and carefully laid him on the sofa, leaving the fence posts in place to minimise the disturbance to the boy who seemed now to be coming round.

The cushions had gone, the blanket was ready, the kettle was boiling.

Chapter 31

The knock on the door made us both jump. We were sitting by the fire with the wireless on, I was reading the newspaper and Mary was darning one of my woollen work socks. We rarely had visitors in the evening: especially in the cold winter evenings each house in the street had its curtains tightly closed, the black outs ensuring that no light seeped out to give away our position to the bombers that still hadn't come.

I looked up at the clock on the mantelpiece, the letter to the Davieses propped beside it, ready for posting in the morning.

Surely all our neighbours were doing just as we were, whiling away the long dark evenings, trying to keep track of the developments in France and Poland and silently praying it would soon be over and not reach us.

The knock was insistent, and Mary put down her darning mushroom onto the arm of her chair and, pressing down her dress with her hands, she made for the door. I knew when she had opened it: I could feel the shard of cold air slicing its way through the gap at the bottom of the door where the draft excluder was no longer in place. And I could hear muttered voices in the hallway.

"Tom!" The voice was still muffled by the closed door but the sense of urgency in it was clear. I can't be sure now if a hundred possibilities went through my head or none, but I leapt from my chair, the newspaper scattering across the floor as it flew from my hands. I threw the door open to see Mary, her hands to her mouth, staring at a ramrod straight woman, dressed in a heavy grey coat, an equally drab grey hat pinned to her combed-back, greying hair. It was the children's headmistress, Miss Tibbut.

"What is it?" I demanded of either, or both.

It was Miss Tibbut who answered. "It's Micky. I've had a call to say he's had an accident. I don't know any details. Something about a hay bale falling on him this afternoon." It sounded for all the world as though she was telling us our boy hadn't done his sums as well as he might.

"A hay bale? How? What was he doing near bales? Who was looking after him? I can't believe Joe would let him there. It must have been Bobby."

"Is he …. all right?" Mary asked the much more important question.

"I really don't know any more than I've told you. The doctor is there but I know no more than that," the frosty woman added.

"We have to go there, Tom," Mary said, still looking at Miss Tibbut.

"I'll leave you to it," the woman said, turning to leave. "Let me know when you have news," she added, and I tried to persuade myself she cared.

Chapter 32

With Micky on his back Dr Garrett again took the boy's pulse and proceeded to run his hands along each of his arms and legs. Though covered in dust Micky was otherwise unmarked. Even the scrapes on the knees which showed below his thick serge shorts, were old play scars. But he groaned and shifted when the doctor concentrated at the top of his left leg.

"I don't want to move him more than I have to," the doctor began, "but I need to see his hip. I think he may have broken it or dislocated it." He gently pushed the trouser leg up as far as he could, and the boy moaned more loudly than he had so far. "There's no blood and no massive bruising yet so I'm hoping the femur isn't broken. But we have to check him at the hospital."

The scale of their responsibility was always clear to Joe and Brenda but since meeting the children's parents the magnitude of it had felt greater. These weren't the children of anonymous, possibly dubious city parents: they had liked Mary and Tom and in turn they had been effusively appreciative.

They waited for the doctor to guide their next move, partly out of respect for his wisdom and knowledge and partly because they had no clue themselves what to do.

Joe had not taken his eyes off Micky and still did not when the Dr Garrett spoke again. "Let's get him into my car. He's small enough to lay on the back seat. If I get him to the surgery, I can get some anaesthetic in him and look at his leg properly."

Joe didn't move or react. He was lost in his tangle of thoughts: fear, guilt, who knew? But certainly, an aching concern for this little charge of his. It was Bobby, again, who took the lead and with a guiding arm round his father's waist he said: "Come on, Dad, you take his head end and I'll take the other. Our stretcher worked fine. The doctor can help when we get to the car."

"Can you give him something now, Doctor?" Joe asked. "It'll be a bumpy ride and I don't want it to hurt."

Even as he asked, Dr Garrett was opening his bag. He took a syringe and pierced the stoppered end of a glass vial with the needle. He upturned them and extracted the contents, withdrew the needle and pressed the syringe's plunger until a thin fountain of liquid sprayed into the air.

With some difficulty and care, moving the boy as little as possible whilst finding the best spot, the dose was delivered to the fleshiest place nearest to the painful hip.

Whilst the painkiller had time to help, they prepared themselves for the walk across the yard to the car which was parked as near as it could be without risk of becoming trapped in pots and ruts.

The short route carrying the boy on a makeshift stretcher was a minefield of potential slips and trips but neither Joe nor Bobby allowed such thoughts to distract them. Bobby turned so that they would both be walking forwards and then looked back to his father. Achieving synchronicity with no more than a look, a nod and the slightest smile, they lifted Micky and made for the door.

Laying him across the back seat was not easy, nor was it without obvious discomfort to the little boy. Joe winced each time Micky moaned or yelped but, somehow, he felt some reassurance when he began to cry and ask for his Mum.

"That's good isn't it, Doc?" asked Joe. "Means his head's okay doesn't it?"

"Possibly," was not as fulsomely positive as Joe would have liked.

Chapter 33

It took me a while to persuade Mary that we could not just set off to get to our son. Heaven knows how much I wanted to, as much as she did, but we had no idea of the train times. We didn't even know how urgent it really was: it may have been that Micky had simply taken a tumble and needed nothing more than a boy-soldier bandage and his Mum to kiss it better.

I knew it was equally possible that it was very serious, but I didn't share that thought with Mary and, instead, did my best to reassure her. We had to sleep on it and hope for more news in the morning.

But sleep on it we could not. We spent the night tossing and turning; trying to sleep; pretending to sleep, in the hope of helping the other to; conceding defeat and holding each other and talking in unnecessary whispers. We got up long before the dawn broke and got dressed for another cold, winter's day, made still bleaker by our concern for Micky.

I had to go to work because there was no excuse for not doing so, though I knew that we needed to be together.

"You come straight down to the factory if you hear anything, Mary. I don't care what they say: if we need to go, we will."

And with that I set off for the factory, trudging through the snow that had fallen over night and which now lay an inch or more thick. My boots screeched as they crushed the virgin white coating but the sounds of voices, doors opening and closing, bottles rattling in milk-float crates were all muted, unlike the ache of worry inside my chest.

Chapter 34

Joe leapt to his feet as Doctor Garrett emerged from his surgery. He felt he had sat there for days, wringing the tweed cap in his hands as though it had just come from the washing and was saturated. Perhaps it was – Joe had held it to his face so many times as he waited. Looking from the door to the ceiling and back again a thousand times, trying to form a prayer to a God he didn't even believe existed. Time had stretched and contracted and lost any sort of shape: Joe couldn't have told you if it was day or night, but he knew he felt an almost crippling tiredness.

He had rehearsed a thousand times in his head what he would say to Micky's Mum and Dad. He tried so hard to say the worst words he could think of but the sentences were never finished because he couldn't contemplate them, let alone say them. Now he found himself looking into the Doctor's eyes, searching desperately for some hint of what he was about to be told.

He looked past Garrett and to the door he had closed behind him. Did he make even the slightest movement towards it?

"The lad's asleep," the Doctor said quietly.

He's alive.

"I've given him something to dull the pain but there's little else I can do. I think he's broken his pelvis but I can't do anything with that, Joe. It just has to heal. It'll take time. Keeping the fella still will be the tricky bit."

"Can't we take him to hospital?"

"Joe, you haven't got the money for that and…"

"I'll find the money, Doctor."

"Joe, I was going to say, they couldn't do much for him there. It's just got to heal."

"Will he be …. you know …. crippled?"

"Can't tell, Joe. He's going to have to stay off his feet and for a little fella that age that's going to be tough. And London isn't …"

"He can't go back there till he's recovered. He has to stay here till he's better." Joe could feel his eyes stinging – tears of worry, guilt, relief. He looked away from the doctor but was glad of the hand he felt on his shoulder. "I shouldn't have let him into the barn. Bobby couldn't have known he'd shifted the bale. I wish I'd told him to stay indoors. How am I going to tell his Mum and Dad? They're such nice people. He's such a lovely lad. Bobby's taken a right shine to him. So have I, truth be told. And he thinks the sun shines out of Bobby."

"Joe, the boy's okay. He's going to be fine. Leave him here where I can keep an eye on him. He's going to hurt and I'll need to help him with that during the night. You get back to Brenda and the kids."

"I'll stop here."

"You won't, Joe. There's nothing you can do and Brenda will want to know. So will Bobby. Alf will run you home in his post van. Now don't argue and get gone."

Chapter 35

We got word from the farm that Micky was very poorly. Hurt. Badly hurt. But alive. The Davieses' message assured us that Micky would be fine, that the doctor said he needed lots of bed-rest while any bone fracture mended. There was nothing we could do immediately and once he came back from the surgery they would look after him well.

I didn't doubt all that but there was no question, we had to go, immediately.

"Tom, we can't afford for you to take time off. There's no saying they'd let you anyway and you can't lose your job." This time it was Mary's voice of reason, but it didn't feel like that to me: it felt as though she was shutting me out. This is a mother's stuff and I was being side-lined.

"You can't go all that way on your own. It's a long journey and it's not right for you to travel all that way. It's not safe. And you might not find it," I explained. "They'll let me take a few days to get you there and back. We can bring Micky back with us so you can look after him here."

"We don't know if he can travel and they won't let you off, Tom. You know the war effort's got you all working double. They'll certainly not pay you, and we can't afford to be without, can we?"

"But…"

"I know you want to see him. I know you want to be there but for now we'll have to manage with one of us and it will have to be me. I'll go on Monday. I can sort out my jobs and go and see him."

"It isn't fair." Even as I said it, I knew it was a feeble, childish thing to say. I didn't really know if I meant it was unfair that Micky had been hurt, unfair that I wouldn't get time off or unfair that I couldn't be with my son. Or was it unfair that I couldn't just say the last of those out loud: simply come straight out and say that I wanted to see him, hold him, reassure him.

"I'll get a message back so you know how he is. I'll be able to ask the doctor when we can get him back here. If we want to, of course. This isn't the best place for him to be, is it? But we'll have to see."

"Oh, he's coming back. We can't expect the Davieses to look after him." If I'm honest I didn't care a jot for the Davieses at that moment – I just wanted Micky and Alice to be at home where they belonged.

Mary set off first thing on the following Monday morning. I walked her to the station, one hand holding hers, the other carrying her case. I waited while she got her ticket, hugged her tightly and watched her go through the barrier and on to the platform.

As I set off for work, I felt more miserable and more alone than I had for a very long time. I missed the children, I missed Mary already. And I missed Nobby. I really missed him. I don't know if I could have told him how I was feeling but he would have known without me saying. He'd slap my shoulder and tell me not to be such a soft tosser. But it would help that he knew, and I needed that, now. I needed my mate so much, right now.

The snow was compacted on the pavements as I trudged home in the dark that first evening and the ground felt as slippery under foot as did my life. When I reached the house and lifted my eyes from the ground for the first time since I left the factory, my heart sank again. Still further.

The curtains were open but, of course, there was no light showing – we had been blacked out since last September in case of the bombers which still hadn't come. But their being open reminded me that there would be no one inside. There would be no fire lit, nothing on the stove, no bath waiting. Just a cold, empty place.

I turned the key and pushed the door open. It felt colder inside the house than out. Silent, still and so very cold. Mary had made up the fire for me to light when I got home but somehow that did nothing but make me feel totally alone. I turned, pushed the door closed, rested my forehead against it, slid to my knees and wept.

I stayed there for who knew how long. But when the tears stopped, I stood, climbed the stairs and, still fully clothed and wearing my coat, I slid under the eiderdown, pulled Mary's pillow into me, drew my knees up and closed my eyes.

Chapter 36

Mary spent the journey looking out of the carriage window, the changing scenery sliding by in a smoky, misty haze of wintery white. When the bus driver greeted her, she didn't hear him say that he was pleased her lad was back at the farm. The bus gingerly rattled and swayed its way towards the farm and she wasn't sure if she was pleased or not to see Joe waiting at the end of the icy lane to the house.

Mary clambered down the steps of the bus and found herself staring into Joe's eyes, desperate for some sort of clue. Had the reassuring message been just a way of easing them towards something more serious?

Joe found Mary's gaze too much to bear and looked down. "I'm so sorry," he said, just loud enough for her to hear.

Mary dropped her case to the ground and her hands covered her mouth to trap inside what would have been a wail. The thump of the case jerked Joe's eyes back to Mary.

"No, no," he began, seeing the misunderstanding etched in her anguished face. He reached out and wrapped his arms round the distraught woman. "No, no, Mary. Micky's fine. At least he will be fine, the doc says. I'm just so sorry it happened. That's what I meant. I'm sorry it happened. I'm so sorry." He could feel the tension in

Mary melt in his arms and he felt sure if he let her go, she would sink to the ground.

When they reached the back door of the farmhouse, Joe with one arm still round Mary's shoulders, her case in his other hand, Brenda was waiting with her arms wide in greeting. It was as though Joe passed Mary over to his wife and the two women enveloped each other.

Suddenly Mary stepped back. She felt guilty that she had accepted the reassuring welcome, without even asking for details about her son. She looked from Brenda, to Joe, to the door that led to the stairs.

"He's asleep, Mary. He's doing fine." Brenda's voice was gentle and warm, in keeping with the kitchen in which they stood – snug, safe, a blanket wrapped round them just as it had felt at Christmas. "I'll get you a cup of tea while you go up and see him. Leave him to sleep and we can tell you everything once you've seen he's okay."

Joe led the way up the stairs and pushed the already open door into Bobby's room. Micky lay on his back in Bobby's bed, lost under an eiderdown which, oddly, didn't show the shape of his body underneath. Mary looked to Joe, puzzled. He leaned towards her and whispered in her ear, "There's pillows each side to stop him turning. Doctor says he needs to be still as possible for a while."

Mary was relieved to see no pain on her little boy's face but it took all her willpower not to scoop him into her arms and run all the way home. Instead she felt Joe's arm across her shoulder again and allowed herself to be turned and guided back down the stairs.

Brenda gestured for Mary to take off her coat. She handed it to Joe to hang behind the back door. Mary sat by the blazing fire as directed and Brenda placed a steaming cup of tea into her hands and sat opposite, next to her husband.

"Can we tell you what happened?" Joe ventured. He was no Believer but he had wondered if telling would be like a confessional and the guilt would be lifted from him. Even just a little would be good.

"Yes please."

"Bobby and me were getting hay for the herd. Micky wanted to come out with us and he was as good as gold: he stayed where I told him to stand. Bobby climbed up to knock the bales down. One got shifted free. It wasn't Bobby's fault. It was my fault. Micky thought we'd finished. I should have made sure he didn't move. I shouldn't have let him come into the barn. He was so good. Bobby was such a good lad: he got the bale off him and went for the doctor. I stayed with Micky. I didn't move him. The doctor says he thinks he might have broken his pelvis but he says he's young and it will mend. With rest. He has to keep still. As long as we can make him. He's sure he'll get better. He will be able to walk again. I should have made sure he was well away. I'm sorry. I'm so sorry."

Joe had hardly taken a breath and without realising it his heavy frame began to shake. He looked to the ceiling: "I'm so sorry," he whispered.

Brenda knew her husband had been carrying this guilt for the days since the accident. It would have been pointless to tell him he had nothing to feel guilty about, but how much she hoped Mary might do that now. There was a silence which lasted longer than she wanted it to. She looked from her husband to Mary, determined not to break into this moment that was not hers to enter.

"Joe," Mary said at last, "Micky was in the barn because you and Bobby were there. He will have wanted to be with you both. I doubt he's ever been happier in his life while he's been here. I just don't believe it was your fault at all. I won't believe it." She paused. "And because he's here with you, at least it wasn't a bomb that dropped on him." She wasn't sure if the attempted joke was for her benefit or Joe's but at least it made Joe look at her. She got up from her seat and put her arms round him.

She was still there when the back door flew open and Alice rushed in, dragging Beckie behind her, the two of them giggling. Recognising the coat leaning over Joe Alice stopped in her tracks before rushing across the room, squealing.

Chapter 37

I wish I could say to anyone who asked that I didn't sleep a wink that night. I shouldn't have, and it made me feel a little guilty that I had slept. My wife was away, my son was lying in a state my own imagination was creating, for want of anything more factual. But I *had* slept, and I woke strangely hot for such a cold morning, until I registered that I was clothed, wrapped in my coat and still covered by the eiderdown. I put my feet to the floor, heaved myself upright, yawned and stretched.

The sleep had done me good and I felt more determined somehow to make everything right again. For months it was as though everything had conspired to take control of my life: Hitler had decided that my home was no longer safe; work meant that I couldn't be where I wanted to be; my closest mate had died because his lungs wouldn't work properly; another family had made my little boy and girl feel happy and free in a way it seemed I could not and that self-same, safe place I had allowed them to go to had caused a hurt that maybe I couldn't mend. But I was now determined to try.

The dark cloud of anguish I realised I had been feeling for months was changing to an anger, the like of which I can't say I had ever felt before. I had to take back control: it was my right, my duty to make decisions. Micky and Alice were coming home. No arguments. No buts. They should be at home with their Mum and Dad, not being looked after by strangers, miles away.

All this bounced around my head as I sloshed the sleep from my face with cold water. I looked around the kitchen: it was neat and tidy as Mary had left it and it was ready to welcome them all back. We could set up a bed for Micky if we moved the table – he'd be warm and no distance for me to carry him out to the privy whenever he needed. I could sleep on the floor beside him if needs be. At least until he was more mobile.

More mobile than what, though? How immobile was he?

I packed a canvas bag with a few things. It would only be a short stay: we were pretty much heading straight back after all, so I didn't need much.

I'll tell the boss that I had to go. He can swing if he doesn't like it. I'll go in tomorrow and travel on Saturday.

Chapter 38

Joe found it hard each morning to leave the house. But since Micky's Mum arrived a couple of days previously, he knew he was looked after and there was nothing he could do. He was relieved Mary didn't look at him with resentment or anger: it helped.

The morning was bright, crisp, clear and for the first time in days he stepped out with a less heavy heart. It had been hard to get Bobby up and Joe knew he was worried for his protégé. But he knew he was uncomfortable with him. Joe had told him over and over that it wasn't his fault but he repeated the 'if only', 'if I hadn't'. Joe told him he had to learn you can't change the past but learn from it and was scolded by Brenda for that. "That's not going to help," she said. "You've just as good as said it *was* his fault." It's not what Joe meant but he was still wrestling with it all himself.

"Hang on, Dad!" It was Bobby calling from the kitchen door and running towards Joe as he struggled into his coat. Joe paused and waited for his boy to catch him up.

"Morning, Bob. To what do I owe this privilege? Last three days I haven't seen you before I've already got the cows in."

"I'm sorry, Dad."

"I've managed."

“Didn’t mean that. I mean I’m really sorry about Micky.”

His head dropped.

Joe took the two steps remaining between them and wrapped his arms around his son and pressed his face into the warmth of his coat.

“Bobby, you listen to me, now. You did nothing wrong. What happened was not your fault. Stacks are always unsteady, no matter how carefully they’re built. I shouldn’t have let Micky get so near and that’s my responsibility, not yours. You were up the top doing the dangerous stuff – all I had to do was keep him safe and I didn’t.”

And so they stood, silently trying to absolve themselves, and each other. And failing. At least now it was a burden shared, a guilt reduced.

Chapter 39

The boss had given me two days compassionate leave so I had today to get there, Monday to get the family ready to travel and Tuesday to get back. I dropped a note through Elsie's door to let her know what was happening and set off.

The journey took hours. The train stopped for no apparent reason between stations. I ignored the other people in the compartment. I think all eight seats were occupied when we left London and I was glad I'd boarded early enough to get a window seat so that I didn't have to talk to anyone, look at anyone. I could just let the miles and the hours slide by.

From time to time we stopped at anonymous stations, the signs having been taken down. My attention would be drawn momentarily to someone heaving their case down from the overhead rack, sliding the door open to the corridor, opening the door to the platform and disappearing through the steam and smoke outside the grimy window.

I must have dozed because eventually, and without me knowing how or when, the other orange, red and brown velvet upholstered seats became empty.

We stopped and started less frequently and I felt I was the only person left aboard as the train rattled, huffed and puffed into the dusk until, finally, it stopped at the little station I just about recognised.

The walk to the farmhouse felt long. It wound its way between the hedgerows I had been able to see over from the bus and it was impossible to know how far I had walked or how far was left. But, at last, the farmhouse came into view.

Smoke billowed from the chimney and soft light glowed from the downstairs rooms I knew to be the kitchen and the front parlour. It looked so welcoming and I had no doubt the children would be sad to say their farewells and leave all this behind.

In the fading light I trod carefully over the cattle grid and headed up the drive to the house. A figure I knew was Joe emerged from the barn to the right. He stopped. He must have seen someone approaching, though I doubt he knew it was me. I had rehearsed in my mind what had to be said and I guessed out there, rather than in front of the women and kids, was best.

"Joe."

"Tom, Is that you? What are you doing here? Why didn't you tell us, I'd have picked you up? Come on in. Come in."

I stopped. Kept my distance. "Not yet, Joe. I've come to take Mary and the kids home."

"Micky can't …."

"Please don't tell me what Micky can or can't do, Joe." I needed to be angry but I was finding it hard. I needed to make clear how careless I thought Joe had been, how angry I was he'd let my boy get hurt.

"But the doctor says he shouldn't move too much and he really couldn't manage the journey to London."

"And we know why that is. He wouldn't be hurting if he hadn't been here, would he? He needs to be home, Joe. I need to have him home."

Joe didn't reply. He should have said something but a silence hung between us instead. I waited for his excuse or at least an explanation that I could reject. But neither was offered and we remained as we were, yards apart staring into each other's eyes through the gloom, like two children weighing the odds before a fight.

I had rehearsed every possible exchange between us during the endless train journey. I hadn't expected silence. I tried to look deeper into Joe's thoughts. Could I see guilt or regret? Was he being dismissive, trivialising it all? It wasn't his boy that was hurt so he was hardly likely to care too much, was he? I shrugged my shoulders, shook my head, looked away and towards the farmhouse.

His voice slid through the crackling cold. "I'm so sorry, Tom."

It was undeniably warm and sincere. So few words but what more did I expect? What more should I need? Probably nothing. I just wanted to take my children home. I offered nothing in return and hoped Joe would turn away and allow me to go to the house. But he stood there.

"Yeah," was all I could say.

"I shouldn't have let the little fella into the barn when we were getting the bales."

"No. I guess not."

"Bob feels guilty about it but I've told him it wasn't his fault at all. It was me who should've been sure Micky kept his distance."

"Yeah, I know."

"Maybe you could tell Bobby you don't blame him."

"Yeah."

Was he waiting for me to let him off the hook too? If so, he'd wait all day.

"Come on, Tom. Let's get in the warm. Micky will be really pleased to see you. You'll need to get him not to move. He has to stay still for …."

"Joe, he'll have to get used to moving so we can go home."

"Tom, he can't …." He stopped himself. Perhaps he'd got the message. I was the one making the decisions. At last he turned and headed for the kitchen door and I followed at a distance. When he reached the house, he opened the door, held it and waited for me. As I stepped inside, the warmth I felt wasn't just the difference the oven made. It was the warmth of a family busy getting a meal ready, talking, sharing. How could all this have been going on so normally when they'd hurt my boy?

Mary was at the sink, her back to me, Brenda at the stove stirring the contents of a pan. Beckie and Alice were arranging cutlery on the table.

"Where's Micky?" It's all I wanted to know. I couldn't be bothered with greetings: I just needed to see my boy.

No one had looked when Joe had come through the door. No one had noticed the door hadn't closed immediately but when I spoke every head looked round, or up. I looked only at Mary who clapped her hand over her mouth.

"I want to see Micky."

"He's upstairs, Tom," Mary answered. "Bob's reading a story to him before tea."

Without invitation, I turned and headed for the stairs and, as I made my way up to what had become the boys' bedroom, I became aware of a hand taking mine. I guessed it was Mary's but I pulled mine away.

"He's doing well," she said. "Be careful he doesn't move too much when …"

"Will people please stop telling me what I can't do, what Micky can and can't do. Will you please let me see him and decide what's best for him? I *am* his dad!"

I pushed the bedroom door open, to see Micky propped up with pillows in Bobby's bed: the mattress beside it had now clearly become the older boy's bed. Bobby sat on the edge of the bed, one leg tucked under the other, his back to the door, reading from the book resting on his lap.

"Hello, Daddy." Micky had noticed me at the open door but instantly turned his attention back to the story. But Bobby stopped reading and jumped up from the bed, clutching the book. 'The Door In The Wall' – Micky's favourite. How ironic: a story about a boy who loses the use of legs.

"Mr Davies … Uncle Tom … Mr …"

"Bobby."

"I'm sorry, I didn't know you'd come. I didn't see you there. I was reading Micky a story. I'm sorry." He paused. "I *am* sorry."

"Could you go downstairs please, Bobby."

He didn't say another word, eased past me through the doorway and headed down the stairs.

"Hello, soldier. How you doing?"

"I'm fine, Daddy. Did you know a big bale of hay fell on me when we were in the barn? We were getting hay to feed the cows. They don't get enough food from the grass in the winter so they have to have extra. Uncle Joe told me to wait by the door and Bobby went up really high. *I* couldn't go that far up. I thought we were only getting one but another one came down. And I went back to be with Uncle Joe and another one came down and walloped me.

"Aunty Brenda says I went to the doctor's but I don't remember that. And the doctor says I have to stay really still for ages and ages until I get better. He thinks I might've broken a bone but he says it will mend because I'm still quite little. Uncle Joe and Aunty Brenda are looking after me and Bobby's let me have his bed. And he reads to me every night. And it doesn't hurt much now. Just a bit when I move. It does hurt a bit when I go to the toilet but Uncle Joe says I have to use a potty for the moment. It's a bit baby but Uncle Joe says it's ok. He says even grown-ups in hospital have to use them sometimes."

"That's all good, Micky. And it gets better. I've come to take …"

"The doctor says I won't be able to go home for a while because that would mean moving and that might mean I can't walk when I grow up. And Uncle Joe and Aunty Brenda say we can stay here as long as I need to. And …."

"But I need you to come …"

"And they said that you and Mummy can come and stay whenever you want to, for as long as you want. How good is that! You can come and stay here, too. That would be like it was at Christmas. That was good, wasn't it?"

Chapter 40

Mary had returned to the kitchen. She felt shut out by her husband but she was trying to understand. He hadn't said hello or pecked her on the cheek and had even snatched his hand from hers. That hurt.

Brenda read the rejection in Mary's face but continued to busy herself with preparing the tea. A few extra potatoes had already been peeled and added to the pan – the ham hock would easily stretch to feed another.

It was Alice who went to her mother and took her hand.

"That was a surprise. To see Daddy, wasn't it?" she said.

"It was. What a lovely surprise." Mary forced a smile. It was a surprise. It was lovely. But she felt anxious, unsure that Tom would listen to reason. She had seen him grow quieter and distant from her over the last weeks but in the minutes since he arrived it was more than that: he seemed almost selfish, unaware, disinterested in her, Alice, possibly even Micky. Fixed on what *he* wanted.

Joe spoke quietly, but not secretively, to his wife, telling her that Tom had come to take his family home. Brenda expressed no opinion but Mary did. "Micky can't travel, can he? The doctor said. Joe you have to tell him."

"I tried, Mary. But he doesn't want to listen to me. And I don't blame him. It was my fault and he knows it."

"It was *not* your fault and he isn't to think that. I'll have to tell him straight and he'll have to lump it!" Mary was surprised by her own vehemence and not entirely convinced by it herself. But she was certain of the need for it and her determination to make her husband see sense.

Tom appeared at the door. He looked deflated: his shoulders hung, he looked to the floor, took a deep breath at just the moment Mary began.

"Tom, you have to listen to me. I know this is hard but just this once I'm not going to give in and you're going to have to hear me out and do as I say. I've never done this before because I always trust you to know what's best but this time *I* do."

"Mary…."

"No, Tom, listen please and don't interrupt. The doctor's been quite clear and explained to Brenda and Joe that Micky cannot be moved. He thinks he'll be fine in the end but only if he moves as little as possible until the damage mends."

"Mary …"

"Tom!" Mary raised her voice and caught herself by surprise. The sound of the urgency in it tripped a switch, the reality of what she had just said came back and she heard it as though it was someone else's voice. "Thinks he'll be fine …. in the end …. damage …." She was determined to finish her demands but now her voice failed her.

"Mary, I know. Micky says he wants to stop here. I suppose it's best."

Tom turned, opened the back door to the yard and walked out, leaving Mary in the middle of a kitchen that wasn't hers, with nothing familiar to pick up and busy herself with. And suddenly feeling very, very alone. She looked around her, not sure if she hoped Brenda and Joe would be there, looking embarrassed by what they had just heard, or there ready to support her. But they had quietly left the room, and Tom and Mary to themselves.

From the front room where they waited Brenda heard the back door. She eased the kitchen door open and peered in. "Can I come in?" she asked, Mary's back to her.

No reply was the all the invitation she needed: she turned Mary to her, wrapped her arms around her and gave her the hug she needed.

Chapter 41

I scrambled over the wooden fence that separated the yard from the meadow at the back of the farmhouse. As I walked, I could feel the gentle incline towards the copse at the far end. It seemed to draw me to it. I didn't know if I would find some sort of protection there, or a gloom which would mirror mine. Perhaps it would simply consume me. I hoped it would.

The dewy grass dragged at my boots and I could feel my feet becoming cold and wet. But I pressed on, until I found myself surrounded by oak and ash and silver birch, tears dripping from their leafless branches.

I tipped my head back to look up. The dull, slate grey sky was visible only in jagged jigsaw pieces through the web of sky-high twigs. And then came a new noise: the howl of an animal in distress or pain, echoing in this bleak room of trees. And I realised it was no animal. It was me.

Chapter 42

It was agreed. Mary would stay at the farm to take care of Micky and ease the burden on Brenda. Tom knew it was right for the boy to have his mother with him and by the summer he would be recovered enough to go home safely, if London could be called safe. Mary and her two would bed down in Bobby's room and Bobby would have a bed made up in the kitchen.

Joe had some misgivings about just how they would cope with yet another person about the place, but at least food wasn't an issue. Yet. But he also wondered how Tom was going to deal with going back home alone and being away from his wife and kids. As the three of them stood in the kitchen making the plans Joe's sharp ears picked up a wailing sound in the distance. It seemed to come from the copse. He couldn't be sure if the women had heard it.

"I'll just pop out and check the fence at the far end of the meadow, Brenda. I'm moving some sheep there tomorrow and I want to be sure it's okay. Don't want that fox getting in."

"Okay, love. I'll have a cuppa ready for you when you get back."

Coat, hat, gloves and boots on, Joe headed across the yard towards where he thought the noise had come from. It had stopped, but he feared he knew the source of the agonising sound. His mind was torn between a need to go there and wondering what he might do if it was what he feared.

Joe crossed the meadow and into the woods. No walls, no door, of course, but he felt the world outside disappear behind him. It was as though he had entered a private place and he was unsure if he was welcome. His boots squeezed the blackened, rotting leaves beneath them as he tramped further into the copse. It became darker, almost ominous.

He stopped. Just ahead, in a small clearing, there was a tree root, a boulder perhaps that he did not recognise or recall. It was neither, but a figure, kneeling, forehead almost resting on the ground.

Joe wondered if he should turn and go, leave Tom to his private torment, stride forward and tell him to pull himself together or stand and wait. He waited. And waited. Until, at last, the broken figure stirred, and Tom's face turned towards him. He heaved himself to his feet like some old, old man and, with shoulders still drooped, he turned and faced Joe. Such exhausted anguish in Tom's face as they closed the gap between them before stopping less than a pace apart. Joe opened his arms as if to say, "What can I do?" and Tom took another step and walked into what he needed to be an embrace.

Awkwardly at first Joe closed his arms round Tom. "Hey there," he said. "It'll be fine, you see." He could feel Tom's face buried in his coat, his shoulders heaving as he silently sobbed.

Time stopped and gradually the peace of the place soothed. Tom suddenly stepped back out of Joe's hold and, looking to his feet, said, "I'm sorry, Joe. Being stupid. I'm really sorry about this, just got a bit too much what with Nobby dying…" his voice caught "… and Micky and that. Stupid. I'm making a fuss. I need to man up. Don't say anything to Mary, will you? Or Brenda. Or the kids, of course. It's just I'm worried. I know it's best for Micky to stay here. And Mary." His voice broke again. "And you have no idea how grateful I am to you and Brenda. The kids love it here. In fact, they love you, you know. You can tell by the way they look at you and talk to you. And I'm glad of that. But it *is* hard to see your kids happier without you and somewhere else than they are with …"

He couldn't say the rest.

"Tom. Stop. Listen to me."

Tom's eyes still stared at the rotting ground beneath him.

"Tom, look at me and listen."

Reluctantly, embarrassed by his display of weakness – God how Nobby would have teased him, Tom looked up.

"Tom, your kids couldn't have a better Dad than you. And your Mary's a saint: she must be to have married you!" Tom smiled and accepted the joke. "They want nothing more than to be with you. That little fella of yours plays with that car you made him every day and you know why?"

"He likes cars," Tom offered.

"No, that's not why he plays with it, you daft bugger. He plays with it 'cause it reminds him of home, of you. Brenda and me are just taking care of them for a while, and I love having them, but they're your kids, not mine and you should be very, very proud of them. And of yourselves for bringing up two such lovely kids.

"You go home and keep things safe there. Mary will look after Micky and come Spring they'll be back home with you. That bastard Hitler will've been sent packing and we'll be back to normal and you can come for holidays here whenever you like."

"But it's such a better life for them here than I can give 'em."

"Oh no it isn't, Tom. It isn't because it's not with their Mum and Dad."

Joe let Tom mull that over and they both became aware of the closing darkness, the eerie stillness between day and night.

"Thanks," Tom said, holding out his hand to shake Joe's.

"Come 'ere, you daft bugger." And Joe wrapped his arms round Tom again.

Chapter 43

The journey home was slow, cold and miserable. I said goodbye to the kids as quickly as I could and all but ran across the yard to the van where Joe was waiting to take me to the station. In my hurry to get away without making a fool of myself again I'm not sure I said goodbye to Mary.

I sat alone in the carriage, my forehead resting on the window which dripped with condensation, and I hoped she understood. When we reached the station, Joe insisted that he would wait until the train arrived – to be sure that it was running – but I needed him to go. I thanked him, apologised for my behaviour the day before in the woods and he just smiled, shook his head and said, "Nothing happened. You look after yourself, Tom, and we'll see you Christmas."

What a difference a year makes. As we rattled along, smoke billowing past the window, smuts landing on the glass, dissolving and dribbling down the pane like melting slugs, I could recall that idyllic Christmas last year. The warmth of the fire, the fill of the feast, the laughter, the easy love in Joe and Brenda's parlour.

How cold the house was going to be when I got home and, as the hours past and I dosed, the dread grew.

The train finally pulled into Euston– on time or late, timetables no longer meant anything. I pulled my bag down from the rack, slid the window down and reached out to open the door. When I stepped onto the platform the air instantly felt thick and heavy. That same cloying gas which had done for Nobby. The ticket collector, huddled inside his black coat, eyes hidden by the peak of his cap, couldn't be bothered to look up as he snatched the ticket from my hand.

The walk from the station to home took perhaps forty minutes. The streets were all but empty. A few shadowy figures ghosted past me, long coats, scarves, gloves and hats hiding every inch of what might be a person inside.

I turned the corner into our street and froze. Not a sliver of light from the blacked-out windows, streetlamps unlit, their dark lanterns boxes barely visible in the swirling mist around them. All there, still whole, but dead. That's me, I thought. For a moment I wished for Hitler to drop one of his bombs right then, right there.

I turned the handle on the front door, stepped inside, closed the door and remembered to fix the blackouts before I flicked the light switch. A weak glow from the bulb in the ceiling hardly penetrated the frigid, dense blackness of the room. The grate was as I left it – a dusting of grey ash over the grate, a mound of it beneath. The scuttle on the hearth was loaded with coal and a bundle of kindling was piled beside it. It could be lit in minutes but I couldn't be bothered. Instead, I dropped into a chair, not mine but Mary's, pulled my coat tighter around me and closed my eyes.

Chapter 44

Brenda and Mary were skilfully manoeuvring round each other in the kitchen when Joe returned from the station. The children were nowhere to be seen, leaving their Mums to get the tea.

The fire roaring in the grate warmed one side of the kitchen, the heat from the stove the other. The room was pooled with a warm yellow glow from the lamps. Gentle rattles of crockery being arranged on the table and the bubbling sounds from the pots on the hob were music to Joe's ears. And above it all, the voices of his wife and Mary chattering to each other as they busied themselves made him feel both content and strangely anxious all at once.

"Tom get off all right?" asked Brenda.

"Yes, no problem."

"Call the kids down for me."

Joe opened the door from the kitchen and called, "Tea's ready, kids."

Within moments the kitchen was filled with babbling and jostling. Micky had woken and Mary sat beside him with hot buttered toast and holding his mug of tea. In the kitchen Joe watched as the children sat at the table. Brenda placed a pile of toast in the centre, a huge pat of butter and a bowl of scorching baked beans, took off her apron and sat herself at the table.

"Help yourselves," she declared. "Come on, Joe, get your coat off and sit yourself down."

Joe looked around the room and felt something he rarely had before. He'd never been to London but chatting to Tom and Mary had given him some idea of what it might be like and he began to imagine what Tom had gone back to. He knew it was not going resemble the scene he was looking on now. And he felt worried: not the worry about whether a sheep would lamb safely, that the crop would be good, that the wood would dry well. But a deep, deep worry for another person. Above all, he felt guilty that he had not done more to help.

Chapter 45

I woke with a start, shivering, aching. The room was pitch dark but there was a hint of something less black at the edge of one of the blackouts – I needed to deal with that.

I heaved myself out of the chair, crossed the room and peered cautiously round the blackout. A grey London dawn had broken with a hint of blue through the broken cloud. Figures were emerging from front doors, coats not quite so closely wrapped around them, scarves a little looser. Another working day. For me too.

I crossed the yard to the privy, then left through the back gate, along the alley to the street and headed for the factory.

The warmth the place offered was good. Some of the women might have asked how things were but I don't recall how I answered. The few men still working there nodded an acknowledgement, but we went to our machines and got on with our work.

The noise was welcome – it filled my head enough to stop other thoughts getting in. Thoughts about my family miles away in the warmth and contentment of the farmhouse; thoughts of my son and what his future might hold; thoughts of going back to that silent house when I clocked off; thoughts of Hitler and what he'd done to my family, without even dropping a single bomb on my city.

"Fancy a pint?" called one of the lads as we clocked off one evening. For a week I'd left work, walked home alone, and gone to bed. I managed on some bread and cheese most days and once the milk turned, I'd persuaded myself that tea was okay without.

"No, thanks. You're all right."

"Come on, just a pint at The Vic."

A log fire roared in the pub's huge hearth, its warmth reaching us as we entered. Candles and lamps provided a welcoming glow and the chatter, the tapping of dominoes, the thwack of darts in the board wrapped themselves around me. A fog of cigarette and wood smoke, mingled with invisible clouds of beery aroma, created a heady concoction. I watched as two tankards of pale ale, topped with a thin cushion of white froth, were placed on the bar. It was hard to recall the last time: was it with Nobby on his birthday? Or was it mine? Or was it when we wet one of our new born's heads? Did we even do that?

"To Nobby," I said and downed the beer, in one.

"I don't need you to take me home. Shod off."

"I'll just see you to your door, Tom. I think you might be a bit out of practice."

"Practish? For what?"

"Come on, mate, you're pissed. I'll get you home."

I do remember turning the front door key, lying on the bed, the room spinning and almost managing to get to the privy before throwing up. Then I must have fallen into a deep sleep.

My head hurt when I woke and I struggled to gulp black, bitter tea. When I got to work no sympathy was offered.

"Morning, Tom. How's your head? You put a few away last night."

"I'm fine. You said I need practice. Fancy another tonight?"

"Sure."

Chapter 46

Life on the farm settled into a contented routine, the addition of Mary making little difference. If anything, Brenda welcomed the company and the help with the chores.

Mary carried the basket of washing into the garden at the back of the farmhouse and, as she pegged it to the line, she became aware that something was different. The sky was lighter, not blue but turquoise and the breeze billowing the sheets was not so cold. She looked across the field to the trees and realised that a lime green haze covered them. The fields were no longer black and sodden.

For weeks her attention had been so fixed on Micky she hadn't noticed Spring creep in. Along the bed that almost surrounded the house, crocuses were cracking open, tall daffodil and tulip leaves reached up, the buds full, ready to burst for want of a few more days of sunshine.

If only Tom could see this, he'd know that all was well. She had written letters to him regularly so that he knew they were fine but she had received nothing in return. It was probably the post in London. Still the bombing was threatened but hadn't started. Many of the children who had come with Micky and Alice had gone home, some of the teachers with them. The village school was happy for Alice to attend.

Micky was stronger each day but still hadn't been on his feet properly, unaided. Joe had taken to getting him to and from the toilet and he'd lifted him in and out of the bath. Doctor Garrett was pleased with Micky's progress but explained to Mary that getting the boy back on his feet was going to be slow and painful. His legs would be weak, his joints stiff from lack of use. But he would give the go ahead to start, quite soon.'

The air warmed, the sun shone, the doors and windows were open more often. London felt a world and an age away.

Once the go ahead was given, Doctor Garrett watched as Joe lifted Micky from the sofa, holding him under his arms. The boy saw the room from a standing position for the first time in three months. And it spun and swam.

Chapter 47

Every night the room spun and swam as I lay down. It wasn't the drink: I was tired and probably hungry.

Occasionally I'd find a pot of stew left on the doorstep for me – probably Elsie from across the road – and I'd eat that, lukewarm. Other days I'd have some bread and cheese. But I didn't need much now the weather was warmer and going to the pub shortened the long evenings on my own. It was the company, not the drink.

That's not true: I usually sat alone in the pub. I reckon Stan got tired of seeing me home and I wasn't much for conversation, I confess.

The days were lengthening and the blackouts weren't needed until later, though I didn't really need mine at all: once I was home, I went to bed.

Mary wrote to let me know how they all were. She said how Joe helped Micky to the toilet and to have a bath and in her last one she said the doctor had given the okay for Micky to start moving a bit. Joe stood him up and Micky said the room was spinning. I hadn't replied: I had nothing to tell her.

July moved to August. More and more kids had come back to London and I hated seeing them playing in the street. Noisy and rude.

"Will you go away down your own end of the street. I'm sick of you banging that ball against my wall."

I was glad when it rained – it kept them indoors a bit more. Unfortunately, early September saw the sun out again and the evenings spent in the pub were as long as ever, before I stumbled home to fall into yet another foggy sleep.

"Shit! What the hell was that?"

My own voice woke me. At least I think it was my voice that did it. I became aware of a ringing sound right inside my ears and distant thuds. The siren we had heard practicing began wailing its ominous rise and fall.

Suddenly a rumbling, crashing noise that I couldn't recognise. Yes, it *was* bells ringing after all, but now they were outside my head. Different, clanging and urgent. A fire. Where? A thud and a boom which shook the room, sending dust scattering and flakes of plaster fluttering from the ceiling.

Despite my grogginess, I leapt out of bed, ran down the stairs and flung open the front door. Opposite, where Elsie's house should have been, was a hole. The roof gaped, the front was missing and the floor between upstairs to downstairs gone. My eyes moved from the pictures hanging at awkward angles on the bedroom walls upstairs, down the exposed stairs, to the pile of rubble opposite me, spewing across the road. It was topped with a bedstead and a bedside lamp, its shade skewed comically.

Water gushed from a pipe pointing skywards, as though desperately trying to wash everything down. The road was littered with broken bricks, roof tiles, shattered chairs and shards of glass, shreds of curtain fabric, strangely unscathed cushions, dented pots and pans.

And Elsie. Bent, crumpled. On her back, arms out, wide startled eyes looking up to where hell had come from.

Too much of her bony, buckled legs was showing from beneath her nightie and I walked over, scrambled up the pile of debris and pulled the hem down to protect her modesty.

I followed her eyes to where she was looking.

"Fuck you, Hitler. You bastard. Elsie made me stew and look what you've done. I fucking hate you!"

Chapter 48

Dr Garrett managed to acquire a wheelchair from a convalescent home in Shrewsbury. Micky was totally lost in the wicker chair, the wooden rim round each of its two spoked wheels too much for him to turn. Joe and Bobby took it in turns to push him into the garden for the fresh air. He would sit there and watch the goings on in the yard; washing being hung and collected in by Brenda and his mother; the sheep and cows grazing in the fields beyond; the clouds scudding across a blue, late-summer sky.

Each morning Joe carried him from the bedroom to lie on the sofa in the parlour and, twice a day, and not without some protest sometimes, onto his feet. At first it really hurt, now it just ached. For weeks his legs felt hollow, wobbly. They didn't have the strength to bear even his meagre weight. But Joe, with more encouragement from Bobby, insisted that everything he did would help him get back to helping on the farm quicker.

Every day Joe would let Micky lie back while he flexed his legs for him, getting the boy to push against him as much as he could.

"That's it, Micky. You try and kick my hand away. Go on. A bit more. Kick harder. See if you can send me across the room." And when he thought Micky had genuinely tried his hardest, he would feign losing his balance and career across the kitchen for Brenda to catch him.

"You daft beggar," she'd say. "Look what you've done, Micky," she'd add as often as the little lad found it amusing.

"You're so good with him," Mary said one evening when the children were in bed and the three adults sat chatting, the radio playing in the background. The windows and the back door were open and the warm summer evening wafted through the room.

"We have to get him strong again, Mary. I want him out of the chair and able to walk by the time Tom comes next." He paused. "Have you heard from him?"

He was not sure why he asked: he knew there had been no word but he could think of no other way of suggesting that he was concerned.

"I expect the factory's so busy. He'll be too tired by the time he gets home. He's not one for writing really." Though on what she based that Mary had no idea and she knew it was an excuse. Sometimes she was anxious, sometimes angry at hearing nothing.

"Shhhh!" Brenda rose from her chair and went to the radio on the occasional table. It was a deep mahogany wooden box, a beige mesh at the front from which the sound came, a glowing dial wrapped across the curve of the front and matching wooden knobs for tuning and volume. She turned one and a rich, sombre voice invaded the room.

"Here is a special announcement. London is under attack. Planes of the German air force, the

Luftwaffe, are bombing the capital. We have this from one of our reporters:

'I can see practically the whole of London spread around me…the whole of the skyline to the south lit up with a ruddy glow…the flames are leaping up in the air now…the dome of St Paul's cathedral is silhouetted blackly against it…it's almost like the Day of Judgement.'"

"Dear God!" Brenda said it before she could clap her hand to her mouth, and regretted it the instant she looked to Mary, who was ashen.

"It's a big place," Joe offered. "They can't hit everywhere." He was no more convinced than the two women. Brenda switched the radio off. "Cup of tea," she said and went across to the stove to set the kettle to boil.

Joe looked at Mary. "Tom'll be fine," he said. "Says they've built shelters and people can go down the underground. They'll have had warning – there are sirens, I think, to warn people to take shelter. He'll be fine, you see."

Mary couldn't find the words to reply. Instead she rose from her chair, climbed the stairs, looked in on Micky before climbing into the bed with Alice and holding her close.

Chapter 49

Daylight brought clarity.

As I opened the door to the street, rubble was already being shovelled onto council trucks, the road made passable. The hole opposite smouldered and steamed like a gaping cavity in a set of teeth. Smoke rose from behind the terrace opposite mine but, despite the gap, it was impossible to see far. The huge metal frame of the gas holder loomed out of the smoke above the roof tops and the church tower close by was still intact.

Elsie had been taken away in the night – who knew where to – and I found myself back in my house to sit all night, often with my hands clamped to my ears to deaden the thuds and cracks. Even as I was glad they were further away, I felt guilty knowing they were landing on someone else.

"Get yourself to the shelter!" the firemen had shouted. "Follow them," they ordered, pointing at the line of families hurrying from their houses and running down the street. But I watched them lift Elsie into the ambulance, went back inside and slumped in the chair. My eyes never closed. Sleep was not welcome or sought. I needed to think. Decide.

Now, in the smoke deadened dawn, my mind was made up. I was not going to shelter, nor was I going to hide in my house. There was only one place I needed to be.

I climbed the stairs, took a suitcase from the top of the wardrobe and packed all I could into it. Once it was full with my clothes and a few more of Mary's, I took the wedding photograph from the bedside table and tucked it between some shirts in the case. The mother of pearl dressing table set Mary's mother had given her nestled inside a pullover and I was ready to go.

We'd never been away for a holiday – last Christmas in Shropshire was as close as we'd ever come to one - but this didn't feel like a trip. A holiday. It felt like goodbye.

Getting a ticket was not as easy as I hoped and the train was busy for most of the journey. Were others getting out while they could? No one asked, few spoke. There was an air of shock about what had taken place. The newspapers declared that this was just the start and London must brace itself for worse to come.

Chapter 50

The following morning breakfast time was subdued. Joe and Bobby had dealt with milking and the six of them sat at the table more quietly than usual, enjoying the endless cups of steaming tea and rounds of hot toast.

Micky sometimes now managed at the table but this morning he stayed on the sofa.

Breakfast done, Brenda set the plan.

"Beckie, will you and Alice go and feed the chickens and get the eggs, please. Bobby you take Micky out for a walk …."

"But Mum…."

"No buts, Bobby. Wheel him across the yard in the chair and then you can walk with him across the field: perhaps he might manage as far as the copse today. What about that Micky? That would be good wouldn't it, if you could manage that?"

In minutes the house was quiet, just Joe, Brenda and Mary sat at the table, the remains of breakfast still uncleared. Brenda placed her hands on the table. "Right, Mary," she said. "Joe, will go down to the village and find out what he can and, if needs be, see if he can phone that woman in London to get some news." She guessed what Mary might be planning and dealt with that. "There's no point in going home, Mary. You don't want to give Tom another worry and it's best if the children don't know what's happened, don't you think?"

"But…"

"You and me can get some chores done with the kids and Joe out of the way," Brenda continued. "Once Joe's got some news, we can think what's best then."

"He'll be fine, you see," Joe said and, taking his cap from the stand by the back door, he stepped outside.

Bobby was racing Micky across the yard in the wheelchair, the two boys making car noises, rasping engines and screeching tyres as they hurtled over the bone hard ground. He watched as they stopped at the gate to the meadow. Bobby moved to the front of the chair to move its footrest aside. Micky reached out but Joe saw a gentle shake of Bobby's head and Micky's hands moved back to the arms on either side of the wicker chair.

He could just see Micky shuffle himself forward in the seat, his feet reached the ground, his elbows bent as he began to lever himself up. Slowly, unsteadily the boy stood. Despite the distance between them, he could see Bobby nodding, grinning from ear to ear.

Micky stood still while his hero walked back round to the handle of the wheelchair and, once Micky had let go of the arms, he moved it backwards, away from him. He re-joined Micky, rested his hand on his protégé's back and Micky took a step forward. His good leg, then the weaker one, then the good one again. He'd managed a few steps indoors with Joe or Bobby steadying him but this was really going solo.

"Mary, Brenda, come quietly and look at this. Shush now though!"

The three of them watched as the two boys began the slow trek across the field. Bobby did no more than keep his hand on Micky's back to let him know he was there, to reassure him, while Micky made his awkward, uneven way over the grass towards the copse.

"It's too far," Mary said.

"He's fine," Joe assured her. "He'll stop when he's had enough and Bobby can carry him back to the chair if needs be."

And with that, feeling prouder of his son than he could have put into words, Joe set off for the village.

Chapter 51

I felt more at ease, more content than I had felt for months. In fact, I *felt* for the first time in months. Numb with tired every day, dulled by alcohol each night I had cushioned myself from loneliness and sadness, so, I suppose love had been dulled too.

But anger had reignited that. No more wallowing in self-pity: anger would have to do for the time being. Worries about anything practical got buried under the rubble on the street: rent, food, job, I didn't care. All that mattered was that in a few hours I would be with my family again. Where I should be.

The train frequently stopped and started without rhyme nor reason. Long, tedious spells spent in sidings were sometimes broken by seemingly endless freight trains rattling past. Other stops came to nothing and we just moved off again, shunting and juddering into the growing dusk.

At last the train slowed and stopped at the Shropshire station I had come to know. It hissed and steamed as though exhausted and just as relieved to be there as I was. Long before we stopped, I had my bag down from the overhead rack, the door window lowered and my hand on the handle outside, ready to turn it and jump onto the platform.

When I did, I was the only person on the platform. Though the light was fading there was plenty of late summer evening to get me to the farmhouse so I set off briskly.

As the walk proceeded, and despite all the hours I had on the train to think things through, it began to dawn on me that I had little or no idea what I was going to do when I arrived. Last time the foiled plan was to take my family home: this time …? I felt I had said farewell to London but there was no place for me here. No work, no room, possibly not even a welcome.

My stride slowed. I stopped, put down my bag and stared across the fields, bathed in an amber glow as the sun dropped behind the hills in the distance. This was a warm, welcome glow from the sky, not that created by flames from burning buildings. I sighed, took up my bag again and strode on.

As I reached the gate to the farm track, ahead of me I could see Joe ahead just passing through the gate to the yard ready to secure it behind him. He stopped. I couldn't be sure if he knew it was me until he waved and called, "Tom?"

I waved back.

"Tom. What the heck? What are you doing here? Come on. Get up here. Good to see you." He held the gate ajar and closed it once I was through.

"Good to see you," he repeated and held out his hand. I shook it. "Come on in. They'll be so pleased to see you. *I'm* pleased to see you."

Joe went ahead of me, through the open back door, calling, "Look who's here!"

In the whirl of noisy greetings that followed I hardly got a word in. Though, in truth, I didn't know what to say. Questions from the children, stories to be told, yet more questions, but all skirting round the real issue. Tea was a bustle of excited chatter between enthusiastic eating of freshly baked bread, cheese, ham, steaming tea and homemade cakes. But still nothing of importance was broached.

One topic was largely avoided for fear of distressing the kids. When Bobby asked, "What were the bombs like?" Brenda smothered it with offers of more tea and another slice of sponge cake. The other topic was totally avoided because it was more complex. What *was* I doing there, in the middle of the week, with a job to do in London, a son now hobbling but not ready to go home – especially to a place now being bombed by the Germans? How long was I expecting to stay and where?

Tea finished the four children were encouraged to make themselves scarce whilst the grown-ups talked.

"So," Joe started. "How are you Tom? You look tired."

"I am. I'm tired of it all. I'm tired of being away from my kids, tired of having no one to talk to at work, tired of having nothing proper to eat, of Hitler. I'm tired of wasting away every evening in the pub."

"No mention of me in that," I heard Mary mutter, as if thinking aloud.

"I'm not *tired* of being without you, Mary. I'm *lost.* It's like my life has fallen apart. A bomb hit Elsie's and there's just a hole there now, a pile of rubble. And that's exactly what I feel like."

"Is she …?"

"Yeah, they killed Elsie. Why Elsie? What in God's name did she do to hurt anyone? She must have just dropped from upstairs to downstairs. I found her lying on top of this mound of brick and timbers and plaster."

Mary, put her hand to her mouth. Brenda's mouth gaped in horror and Joe shook his head. The image hung in the air until Joe broke the silence.

"What's your plan, Tom?

A simple question which exposed the fact that I didn't have one. I had abandoned the house and work, set off, clear in my mind where I wanted to be. But Joe was right – I needed a plan and I didn't have one.

"I don't have one, Joe," I admitted. "I needed to be here and, I guess, I needed to get away. Suppose that's cowardly? I mean, I can't fight them and now I'm not even helping the ones that can."

No one spoke. I was right. I was nothing more than a coward, running away, risking my job: useless.

We sat for a while, avoiding each other's eyes, searching, I assume, for a way to say what had to be said. Go home and get on with it. Simple as that. But not so simple. At last Mary and I caught each other's gaze. I knew she'd say what had to be said: she was stronger than me, in truth, but she would choose her words carefully. She opened her mouth to speak.

"It's probably not for me to say but I have an idea." It was Joe's voice, not Mary's. The three of us looked to him. I was relieved, Mary possibly irritated at being interrupted and Brenda curious. She placed her knitting on her lap: she knew to wait.

"It's just an idea," Joe repeated. "But it might work. Let's just sleep on it, give me a bit of time tomorrow morning and maybe by the afternoon I'll tell you what I've got in mind."

"A hint?" Brenda asked but didn't push the point when Joe did not reply. It wasn't for me to ask.

Chapter 52

Sleep came remarkably easily for Tom, crushed against Mary in the single bed they shared for the night. It was bliss to have her warmth next to him for the first time in weeks. It soothed, comforted, reassured and he quickly slipped into a deep sleep.

Mary did not. She lay still, pleased to have Tom there beside her but only drifting in and out of sleep. Each time she woke another worry invaded her mind: she tried to resolve it, usually unsuccessfully, dozed again, only to wake with another trouble. When she managed to block out those worries it opened up a hole for her to worry for Micky.

He was recovering remarkably well, moving about on his own, good tempered and patient with his limitations. But Mary was very conscious of the limp, the lopsided, awkward walk. When he had tried a short run after a wayward hen it would have been comical had it not been sad and a worry. What, she wondered, did her son's future hold? How restricted would he be as he grew? Would he attract a wife, get a job?

When she woke again, Tom had already gone from the bed. Mary followed her usual routine, getting herself up and dressed before rousing Alice and dealing with Micky. It was no surprise that Joe was not in the kitchen when everyone gathered for breakfast but it *was* odd that he still wasn't there by the time they had finished and almost cleared away. Bobby came in having dealt with the cows.

"Your Dad on his way?" Brenda asked.

"Not sure where he is, Mum. He went off and left me to clear the shed after we'd milked. Said he had to go and see someone. He went over Yockerton Hill towards Mrs Crockley's place."

Brenda stopped her pot-washing, hands still in the soapy water in the butler sink, and looked through the window across the yard. It was a bright, clear day. The sky was already a deep blue, almost cloudless. It would be warm soon. A perfect late summer morning.

A smile. A gentle shake of the head and she returned to her washing up.

Chapter 53

When Joe finally reappeared, I wanted desperately to ask him what I should do but he brushed off any attempt I made to talk to him. He was busy, he got me busy, helping him with various chores and instructing me as though I might sometime do it all again. This needed to be there, that here, always be sure to do this, that or the other so the cows don't get sick. Shake the hay loose, make sure the water trough's full and clean, wash down the yard.

I confess I enjoyed the physical work in the fresh air, and I was surprised that my back ached less than when I was stooped over the lathe. But, fascinating though it was, I really didn't need the detail! I didn't have the heart to stop him. In fact, I liked hearing his voice: it was reassuring and I think I was somewhat in awe of his knowledge and wisdom.

By the time Mary came to the door and called us in for something to eat, I was part relieved for the break and part disappointed because I knew the spell was about to be broken. Reality had to be restored. I would be going back to London.

Three children ate fast, through a blur of chatter but Bobby was quieter. I guessed he might feel resentful of someone else muscling in on his status as number two, even for such a short time. He had been busy repairing hen houses while Joe and I had worked together. He probably felt pushed out. As

I was looking at him, mulling this, Bobby caught my eye and, instead of scowling or looking resentful as I expected, his face lit up. He beamed. He must be so glad I was going.

"I am sorry, Bobby. I'll be away really soon." He laughed.

"Bobby!" Joe's correction was sharp but nowhere near as fierce as I would have expected. Bobby's Dad must be just as pleased to be seeing the back of me.

Bobby looked away and I pushed my chair back, certain that I should go and pack my bag.

"Hang on, Tom." Joe had seen me move. "Kids could you scuttle off and play so that the grown-ups can have a chat?"

Without a pause, with no argument the four children went to get up from the table, "Not you, Bobby," said Joe. At that Becky hesitated but Brenda smiled and nodded to her and that was enough. Brenda cleared the table and began to wash the dishes but Joe asked her to leave them and sit back with them.

"I'll get my bag packed. Perhaps you could run me to the station," I began.

"I have an idea to put to you," said Joe, ignoring me. "I went to see Doris Crockley this morning. She has the farm over the other side of the hill: our back field joins onto her Long Meadow. Her husband Reggie died last year and she's been struggling with the farm. Her boy joined up and he was pretty useless on the farm anyway, to be honest. He and his father didn't get on easily. Worse than you and me, Bobby!"

Bobby grinned at his dad. It was as though he was in on some private joke.

"I've been giving her a hand when I can," Joe went on. "Not a lot: there's a fair bit to do here so I can't help much. And her place is not going too well now. The barns need some work; the yard's a mess; the house is way too big for her to manage and needs a lick of paint, and the machinery she's got desperately needs looking after. So does mine for that matter. If we don't get that cultivator fixed, Bobby, we're going to be in a right mess."

I knew I had to hear the story out. Joe was too kind for me to be impolite.

"Joe, to the point eh?" Brenda prompted, though what point I had no idea, and really wanted to get away now.

"Oh yes. Well, I went to have a chat with her this morning, to put an idea to her. To say she was keen is a bit of an understatement. Brenda, she hugged me so tight I could hardly breath. She's such a lovely lady, isn't she? She really doesn't deserve to …."

"Joe!" Brenda interrupted again.

"Right. Yes. I suggested to her that she might like a manager to look after the farm for her. The house is plenty big enough for a family to move in. The farm would be hard work, especially to start with because it's been a bit neglected but, Tom, I reckon you could do it. With help from me and Bobby, here."

Try as I might, I'd almost stopped listening, waiting for Joe to finish his story but the mention of my name had caught my attention again.

"Do what, Joe? Help with what?"

"Help you manage the farm. You don't mind hard work – I saw that this morning. Micky needs to stay here for the time being to help him recover and we can get him and Alice registered at the school properly. Mary could help Doris get the house sorted, you could run the farm, and Bobby says he'll happily go over there to help, especially to start with."

"I can lend a hand with the house, Mary," Brenda offered. "We'll get it spick and span in no time. Doris is a lovely woman: you'll like her I'm sure of that."

I opened and closed my mouth several times before any words came out. I'm not sure what they were when they did. It was Mary who managed to talk some sense: she who started to explore the practicalities of both the farming and the house arrangements. As the brain fog cleared, and I persuaded myself that this was a genuine plan, my questions began. They were all negative: not because I didn't like the proposal, more that I couldn't believe it could really happen.

"What about the house?" "What about my job?" "What about the kids' school?" "What about Julie?" I had hardly given a thought to Julie: it was Nobby who had been my friend, not her. I had left her to get on with things without him, and that was unkind. Selfishly, I didn't want to imagine a hurt greater than mine but she must miss him even more than me.

To each of my questions someone had an answer. The Crockley farm was viable and not completely neglected. It generated an income which would support a family, even as it was, but had the potential to earn more. Joe took the view that, if the two farms worked together on some things, they could both thrive.

He spoke about acreage and crop-yield; fallowing, rotation and grazing; efficiency and economies of scale. Of course, Joe must know his stuff but it was business talk and, frankly, it scared me. I knew nothing of either business or farming and little in my life had been planned: things happened and I dealt with them as best I could at the time. Sometimes not very well, I admit. This was about the future at a time when the world itself might not have one.

"Let's do it, Tom. What's to be lost?" Mary's face left me in no doubt that I had no option.

Chapter 54

An agonisingly long journey took Tom in Joe's van back to London to gather the last few things from the house. Joe was very quiet as they drove to the house, past piles of rubble that were once houses – gaps in the street like more extracted teeth. He felt almost embarrassed, as though he were looking at someone caught naked – possessions exposed, wallpaper pealing from walls that would not normally be seen, even the occasional lav in houses which had one fitted indoors.

The van was loaded and they headed back, driving through the dark with the headlamps all but useless with the hoods over them that Joe had constructed and fixed on. Once they were away from the city they came off and the going was a little easier. They drove past the farm, on to Crockley's, where they unloaded the things into a barn, ready for moving in the next day.

And the next morning Doris was whole-hearted in her welcome, showing Mary the kitchen while Alice explored the house. Joe and Tom carried the things from the barn and the few items they had at Joe and Brenda's were brought in. Doris had it all planned: the front parlour was theirs, the children had a room each and she had moved her things to the smaller of the other bedrooms to give Tom and Mary the double.

No matter how hard Mary insisted that this was not right, Doris brushed it off and insisted that, without this plan, she would have to sell up and she really couldn't contemplate the idea of leaving the farm.

"It's where Reggie is," she explained, and Mary understood.

"It still doesn't seem right for you to be squashed in there," Mary pressed. But she would have none of it: she had already moved her things and had no intention of moving them back.

With everything sorted, their furniture (which had filled their little living room at home) was lost in the parlour. The beds were made up and it was time to get Micky. He was now walking more but he still needed the wheelchair some of the time. It waited in the kitchen.

Before Tom could make the trek across the field to collect his son, he spotted Joe walking across the yard with Micky on his back. Joe was talking, Micky laughing.

Chapter 55

I felt a stab of jealously but it passed when Joe called out: "Delivery for Crockley's Farm! I'll take it away if no one wants it!"

"I'll have him," I replied.

"He's a bundle of trouble you know. You sure you really want him? I can't wait to get rid of him, can I fella?" Joe shook himself and Micky giggled.

"I reckon I can cope with him. Now."

"I'm reckoning you can," said Joe, an uncommonly wide smile lighting his face. "I'm reckoning you can."

Mary came to the front door, beaming as she beckoned the delivery man and his 'parcel' into the house.

And so began our new life. Mary and Brenda, with Doris's approval and help, set about reorganising the kitchen to cater for a family. Mary could not at first understand why any woman would allow such a total take-over but it soon became clear that Doris really welcomed the company and the feeling that the farm, and her home, were safe.

Joe spent hours each day for the first weeks guiding me around the farm chores. At first, I could not quite believe what was happening, then I felt excited by it all. Sometimes, as we sat in the evenings, I dared to share with Mary my fear of failing. I can't do it, I would say.

Everything will go wrong; the animals will fall ill; the crop will surely fail; the farm building fall into wrack and ruin. But Mary would reassure me, and I suspect she secretly asked Joe to encourage me some more.

As the weeks past I found the routine easier, the rewards greater than the worries and sessions spent with Joe talking about seed and fertilizer needs for the two farms made more sense. Gradually Joe came less to help and guide and, instead, Bobby would appear when it was agreed there was a two-handed job that needed doing.

Alice tripped off to school each morning, regaling us each evening with what her new friends had done and said. Soon came the requests for them to come for tea.

Micky spent more and more time out of the wheelchair and, after some time struggling with some crutches the doctor brought from the hospital, he managed to walk with a stick, then unaided. He would hold tightly to my hand as we walked across the yard to fetch the eggs and I knew he'd really come back to me. He walked with an uneven gait and we began to accept that he would always walk with a limp. He never complained but every now and then we would catch sight of him grimace. But the pain, such as it was, was neither severe nor prolonged and when it was clear that he was strong enough, he too scampered off to school enthusiastically.

London was a world away.

But he would tire by the end of the day. The effort of walking and then trying to run with his friends wore him out. Joe had carried a bench from the yard to the bottom of the garden, overlooking the fields and I would often sit with Micky after school while he rested before tea.

Sometimes we would talk about school, sometimes about the farm. Sometimes we just sat in silence, my arm round his shoulder as he snuggled beside me.

Hitler was an irrelevance. As Mary and I sat in the evening, I would happily have turned the wireless off when the news broadcast began but she insisted that we keep ourselves informed. We heard of the bombs raining down on London; the fires; the destruction; the families huddled under their stairs or running through the streets to the nearest underground station. It made me feel relieved and guilty at the same time.

One evening when I went to turn the wireless off Mary said, "We need to know what's going on at home, Tom."

Without thinking and without a doubt in my mind, I replied, "But Mary, this *is* home."

Epilogue

"Grandad. Tea's ready. I'm surprised you haven't worn that bench out! You sit there every single day.

"It *is* a lovely view, and I bet it hasn't changed much in all the years you've sat here and looked at it. Who put it here Grandad, the bench I mean? Was it your Dad?

"Was it when you hurt your leg?

"Have you dropped off to sleep, Grandad?

"Grandad.

"Wake up, Grandad. Please wake up, Grandad"

About the Author

Keith Stuart (Wadsworth) taught English for 36 years in Hertfordshire schools, the county in which he was born and has lived most of his life. Married with two sons, sport, music and, especially when he retired after sixteen years as a headteacher, travel, have been his passions. Apart from his own reading, reading and guiding students in their writing; composing assemblies; writing reports, discussion and analysis papers, left him with a declared intention to write a book. Pied Piper is 'it'. Starting life as a warm-up exercise at the Creative Writing Class he joined in Letchworth, it grew into this debut novel.

Printed in Great Britain
by Amazon

77178240R00113